I MARRIED A MERMAN

Prime Mating Agency

REGINE ABEL

COVER DESIGN BY
Regine Abel

Copyright © 2022

CONTENTS

I MARRIED A MERMAN

She belongs to a different world.

Struck by a strange illness that confounds human doctors, Neera turns to alien physicians instead. The prognosis? She's not what she always believed herself to be—Earth's atmosphere is slowly killing her. Too broke to afford the insane cost of relocating to a new, more suitable world, Neera turns in desperation to the Prime Mating Agency. The match? A sexy merman, with pink scales, scarlet hair, and a voice that makes her toes curl.

When Echo hears the Agency has finally found a match for him, he's over the moon. Finding out his mate's weakened health will require much caring and nurturing during her recovery has his protective instincts surging forward. Despite some initial awkwardness, her courage, resilience, and mischievous personality have him enthralled.

But as Neera evolves into her true self, will this newfound haven become toxic for her as well? Will she be forced to leave behind the blossoming happiness she has found here with Echo?

DEDICATION

To all the medical professionals who go out of their way to alleviate our suffering, to give us hope, a better quality of life, and the answers about this complex and mysterious wonder that is the human body.

To those who have or currently are suffering from chronic illnesses and pains, who put up a brave front every day to carry on with their lives, who refuse to surrender or be defeated. Remember that no matter how dark the night, the sun eventually always rises.

CHAPTER 1
NEERA

The hovercab came to a stop in front of the tall building that once served as a quarantine facility more than 300 years ago. It looked nothing like that now thanks to its high walls made of white stone and the high-tech upgrades it had received over the years. Today, it served as an alien research center called ARA. I didn't know what the letters stood for. The words were in a foreign language.

Desperation brought me all the way here and convinced me to put my fate in the hands of people from another world. I had no other choice. Traditional human medicine had given up on me, failing to find the cure to my debilitating condition.

I paid the driver, cringing at the—unsurprisingly—steep cost of the ride, considering how isolated the facility was. With my meager finances—struck all the harder by constantly mounting medical bills—I had to save every penny where I could.

Nothing stood out about the typical corporate entrance of the building. Tall glass doors opened on a relatively fancy greeting hall and security desk. A single human male occupied it. As soon as I approached, he smiled in greeting.

"Ms. Michaels, welcome to ARA. Dr. Meri Atani is waiting for you."

My eyes widened in surprise. Did they have so few visitors that he automatically knew my identity, or had Dr. Patel sent my full file including my picture beforehand?

"I will open the security doors. Simply go through and follow the corridor to the end. The doctor will be waiting for you," the guard said.

I thanked him, feeling somewhat unnerved by the process. The thick set of doors, the type you'd expect to see barring the entrance to a bank vault, slid open quietly. It revealed a long and wide corridor, with gleaming white walls and pale blue tiled floors. The place was spotless with a light scent of bleach and lemon. As soon as I entered it, I felt the air around me shift. It was subtle yet undeniable. That didn't stop me from advancing further. As I neared the end, the hallway opened up to a large circular room. A female with a white lab coat stood a couple of meters away with a welcoming smile on her alien face.

Although Earth now hosted a handful of alien species—either as permanent residents, traders passing through or temporary visitors—I'd never seen this specific one. She possessed an exotic beauty. The long light-gray dress under her coat covered most of her humanoid body. If not for her facial features, the odd texture of her hair, and her fin-like ears, she might have passed for a human. Her skin was light blue, and I could see some scales peeking through her square collar. Although not flat, her nose wasn't as pointy as a human's and the nostrils were far smaller. But it was her midnight blue eyes, locked on me, that held my attention. She blinked and, after her eyelids reopened, a horizontal set closed and opened over her eyes, the same way the nictitating membrane did with certain lizards.

For some strange reason I couldn't explain, I instantly liked her and almost felt like I was meeting an old acquaintance, which made no sense whatsoever.

"Hello, Ms. Michaels. Welcome to the ARA Research Center," the female said. "I am Dr. Meri Atani, and I will look into your case today."

"Hello, Dr. Atani," I said with a nervous smile. "No pressure, but I'm certainly hoping you'll be able to perform some miracles for me."

The sympathetic smile she gave me stirred an uneasy feeling deep within. Maybe it was just paranoia after so many deceptions, but I instantly got the vibe that she already knew she would not be able to help me and was merely going through the motions.

"This way please," she said, gesturing towards the left side of the large room. "We will be a lot more comfortable speaking in my office."

I followed her, discreetly slipping a finger under my mask to loosen it a little. My face had become bruised from excessively using it of late. To my chagrin, the doctor was walking too briskly. Keeping up made me exert far more energy than I wanted to. In no time, I was feeling out of breath as—by design—my mask limited my oxygen intake to prevent it poisoning me. Thankfully, her office wasn't too far away. A part of me silently berated myself for not merely asking her to slow down. You'd think after all this time I'd be beyond this type of silly pride.

We entered her office, and she pointed at the comfortable leather chair in front of her desk. It struck me as odd that there would be a single chair when they usually had two for whoever accompanied the patient. Then again, how often did actual patients come to this alien place?

I cast a nervous glance at the examination table. I'd never seen one specifically like this one, but it clearly doubled as a medical pod. Although I doubted it could perform very advanced procedures, it could likely do basic surgeries as well as advanced scans and MRIs.

"So, Ms. Michaels, I have received your file from Dr. Marnie Patel regarding your breathing issues. I have consulted it extensively and performed my own analysis on the blood and tissue samples she forwarded to our facility. However, I would like you to explain to me in your own words how it all began, what your current symptoms are, and what measures you are using to mitigate them."

I squared my shoulders and launched into the story I was tired of repeating. But for the first time in forever, I actually held some hope of a more positive outcome.

"About a year ago, I got a fever that lasted for a few days, with body aches and headaches. It felt like having some sort of flu without the runny nose or the coughing. Then overnight, the fever and all the other symptoms disappeared, and my throat would mildly tickle whenever I inhaled. After a few days, it turned to frequent coughing. As it occurred in the spring, I figured maybe I'd suddenly developed some sort of allergies."

"Were you diagnosed as having allergies at that point?" the doctor asked.

"The first doctor I saw said yes. The second wasn't too sure.

But the third doctor said no," I replied with a dejected expression. "Anyway, the anti-allergy medication I'd been prescribed did nothing for me. And then things got really bad. My lungs burned whenever I inhaled, and I experienced uncontrollable coughing and shortness of breath. That's when Dr. Patel said that I was displaying all the signs of oxygen poisoning. She gave me an oxygen control mask to try out. It helped a little at first, but I still experienced tunnel vision, tinnitus, nausea, and waves of dizziness. I really freaked out when the seizures started happening followed by waves of spasms. The doctor then confirmed that I was indeed suffering from oxygen toxicity."

"How did she treat you?" Dr. Meri asked.

"They placed me in an isolation room with strictly controlled oxygen levels," I said, my eyes going out of focus as I remembered those terrible days. "I remained there for nearly three weeks while my symptoms faded, and I slowly recovered. I then had to purchase the mask I'm currently wearing. Although it doesn't fix my problem, it allows me to function in a limited capacity. But I feel like I'm constantly suffocating because it reduces my oxygen intake. I also had to invest in turning my apartment into a pressurized room to control oxygen levels within."

The doctor nodded, seeming totally unsurprised by everything I was telling her. That gave me further hope that she knew what was wrong with me and how to fix it.

"This aligns with what Dr. Patel has described, and what I expected based on the analysis of your samples," Dr. Atani said.

"So, you know what my problem is? You know how to fix it?"

Once more, she gave me that sympathetic look upon

seeing the eagerness—not to say the desperation—on my face and hearing it in my voice.

"Yes, Ms. Michaels. I know what the problem is," she confirmed in a careful tone. "Before I continue, I would like to ask you a question that you will probably find odd. But please indulge me."

Stunned, I nodded nonetheless for her to proceed.

"Tell me, Ms. Michaels, are you unusually passionate about either swimming or flying?"

I gaped at her, getting whiplash from the complete change of topic, while wondering what the heck that had to do with anything.

"Swimming," I finally answered, although my voice hid nothing of how baffled I felt. "I've always been obsessed with water. I planned on becoming a marine biologist, but my health has pretty much derailed my studies and my life as a whole."

The doctor smiled and nodded. "It is not surprising. I suspected as much the minute you walked in." She chuckled at my baffled reaction to her comment. "My words confuse you right now, but I'm about to explain a few things to you that will likely blow your mind. I just need you to bear with me, and all will be clear in a moment."

I nodded again, this time feeling restless, curious, and somewhat worried.

"Before I do, I would ask you to remove your mask. It's okay," she added when I looked at her with an air of panic. "You probably felt a shift in pressure when you entered the hallway leading here. This entire section, past the security desk, is pressurized differently, in a way that you should find very comfortable. My people, the Sikarians, do not mingle with humans for this very reason. We would die from oxygen poisoning in Earth's atmosphere."

Despite my fear, I complied, trusting the female in a way I couldn't quite explain. As soon as I removed my mask, I could have wept with relief being freed of the painful pressure it exerted on my face. Even removing my bra when I got home didn't feel half as amazing as this. I took a couple of tentative breaths, expecting the brutal cough to resume within seconds. Instead, it was as if a heavenly light had invaded my lungs in oxygen form. Tears pricked my eyes as I carefully breathed in.

"I had forgotten what it felt like," I whispered with a trembling voice. "Even at home it isn't this perfect."

"This area has been specifically calibrated for you," the doctor said. "It is actually not ideal for me, but not uncomfortable. It will not harm me to stay here for the duration of our meeting."

"Are you sure?" I asked, worry slipping into my voice.

"I am. But now, time for some explanations. Do you remember the 2006 pandemic called the Arctic Fever?" Dr. Atani asked.

I recoiled again, thrown once more by another completely weird question. "Vaguely. It was mentioned in our history classes as being one of the strangest events to hit human history. But that was 300 years ago."

"Correct. Global warming caused the Arctic Fever, named this way because the virus originated from the poles. As the permafrost melted, it released into the air, soil, and groundwater dormant microbes containing prehistoric enzymes. A very small percentage of the human population was vulnerable to them and became sick. Most people quickly recovered on their own while others needed some treatment. But in an even smaller number of cases, the release of three specific viruses caused a mutation in certain genetic codes."

"I never heard that," I said in a dubious tone. "We were told that although the disease hit every country worldwide, only a small percentage of people contracted the disease. And an even smaller number—albeit smaller is a relative term—actually died from it."

"They did not die," Dr. Atani corrected. "They mutated."

"Mutated into what?" I exclaimed, flabbergasted.

"Mutated into one of us, as you were always meant to be."

My brain tilted, and I stared at her, robbed of words.

What the hell does she mean by that?

"I know you're lost right now, but I will explain. My people, the Sikarians, have been explorers and settlers for millions of years. Among many other planets, our ancestors settled on Earth. Unfortunately, only a few years after their arrival, the meteor that wiped out the dinosaur also massacred the settlers. Back in our homeworld, they thought everyone had been lost. It took nearly 60 million years for us to even look back at this planet, only to find that some of our people had survived, mostly the Thalans, one of the three breeds that had settled here."

"Three breeds?"

"First, there are the Thalans, like you and I, who are water creatures. Then there are Khilzains, who have more draconic traits. And finally, the Elohim, who are the most human in appearance and who are often confused with angels. The survivors evolved differently on this new planet, especially once they started mating with the homo sapiens. And thus was born the human race as we know it."

I snorted and shook my head in disbelief. "Hold on. Let me get this straight. You're trying to tell me that your ancestors came to Earth millions of years ago, had babies with our cavemen, that I'm one of their descendants, and that some virus is making me turn back into one of you?"

She chuckled then nodded. "I know it sounds crazy when you summarize it like that, but it is the truth. I have nothing to gain by lying to you about this."

She turned on a holographic display at the edge of her desk, which allowed us both to view the screen. On it, she played a video showing various humans going through phases of mutation. By their original clothes and hairstyles, they clearly dated back to the early 2000s.

"These are some of the people who went through that transition and moved to our ancestors' homeworld. Why did we hide it from the population, you wonder?" she asked. I nodded, stunned. "Back then, as Earth was still considered a primitive planet, it fell under the restrictions of the Prime Directive. Therefore, we couldn't let the general population be aware of our existence."

"But our governments knew, didn't they?" I asked.

"Yes, they did. We entered into an agreement with them so that our awakening people wouldn't be treated like freaks and turned into lab rats," Dr. Atani explained. "And that brings us to you. You are suffering from oxygen poisoning because your lungs have partially mutated and want to breathe like a Thalan. But this planet does not allow it."

"Are you saying I have to leave Earth and settle with you guys on your planet while I turn into one of you?" I asked, feeling surprisingly excited rather than terrified.

The doctor hesitated, a troubled expression crossing her alien features. "You indeed have to leave Earth. Remaining here will slowly but surely kill you," she answered cautiously. "However, you cannot come to Sikaria. You see, this facility has taken the front of a research lab for the very rare cases like you that still pop up from time to time. It allows us to provide our awakening people with a safe environment to complete their mutation before we take them home. But normally, when the gene awakens, the mutation occurs smoothly over a period of five to eight weeks. Your evolution has been stalled for over a year."

"What do you mean? I'm not going to fully mutate? I'm stuck?" I asked, my throat tightening.

My heart broke at the sight of the sympathetic expression on her face. "You are in what we could call limbo. Your mutation evolved in the wrong direction then stopped. Based on my analysis and study of your medical history, I believe that your mother's substance abuse during her pregnancy with you is responsible for the issues you currently face. Unfortunately, we have no way of knowing whether your mutation will resume, how far it will go—if it does at all—or if you will remain this way forever."

I swallowed hard, refusing to admit what her words possibly implied. "But... but why can't I go to your planet to wait and see if the mutation resumes?"

"Because our atmosphere would be just as deadly for you as Earth's currently is. You are no longer human, but not yet Sikarian. That said, there are other planets that have the type of atmosphere where you would be able to thrive while we assess how your situation evolves."

I ran nervous fingers through my hair as I took in her words. "Okay... Are you going to send me there like you did with the other humans that mutated?"

My heart sank when she gave me an apologetic smile.

"Unfortunately, we cannot take you on as you are not offi-cially one of us. Your situation will require a lot of tracking for who knows how long, maybe your entire life if your transformation never triggers. We cannot take on such a responsibility for edge cases like yours. I can give you a list of planets where you could go, including the name of a few contact people. But you will have to arrange that relocation on your own."

I stared at her disbelievingly. "Are you serious? Interstellar travel is insanely costly. And I bet the planets you're referring to are not even in one of our neighboring solar systems. I can't afford that. I grew up in an orphanage and then went from one foster home to the next. Just when I was starting to get somewhere, this stupid mutation wrecked my life and put me on the verge of bankruptcy. And now you're telling me it sucks to be me and to figure it out?"

"I empathize with your situation, Ms. Michaels," the doctor said in a sympathetic tone. "Sadly, my hands are tied on this. I do not have a budget to relocate people elsewhere. Our government sends a ship to recover Sikarians here and bring them home, that's it. But there may be an alternative for you."

"Alternative?" I asked, bracing for yet another disappointment.

"There are ways for humans to travel off world at no cost. While you would not qualify for most of the programs, there is one thing you could do. Would you consider the PMA?"

"The what?"

"The PMA, the Prime Mating Agency."

"Right... I remember them now. But you want me to marry an alien? Why would anyone want someone as busted up as I am? Even my fellow humans won't give me the time of day!"

"You would be surprised, Ms. Michaels. And you're not

busted up, you are merely in limbo. Do not forget that the Temerns run that agency. Thanks to their empathic abilities, they will pair you with someone that is a perfect match for you, and in a world that would be suitable to your needs."

Although still shocked by that prospect, the Temerns held a stellar reputation when it came to moderating contracts, peace treaties, and any other form of agreement. Their empathic abilities allowed them to assess the emotions of all the parties involved. Therefore, businesses and governments alike highly sought out their services. Surprisingly, the Temerns also headed that matrimonial agency, which focused on finding compatible partners for primitive aliens, not for advanced worlds.

"We have a few sister worlds, Sikarian colonies that have evolved differently from our own world. There are at least three of them on the list I will provide you. Their atmosphere would be great for you, and you would still be with our distant relatives. Through the Prime Mating Agency program, every-thing would be handled and paid for by them at zero cost to you. If things go wrong or if you start mutating and are no longer able to remain on that new planet, the PMA will be responsible for finding you a new home."

Feeling overwhelmed, I didn't know what to say or what to think. I only knew that I could no longer live like this or it would kill me.

"Listen, Ms. Michaels, here's what I can do for you," Dr. Atani said in a gentle voice. "Let me contact the PMA for you and explain your situation. One of their agents will come interview you so that they can assess your personality in order to find the perfect partner for you. You are under no obliga-tion to marry that partner once they find one, but at least you will have that option. I cannot say how soon an agent can see you or find you a match. However, I could let you stay here for two weeks—maybe three weeks maximum—to help heal your lungs and central nervous system in the meantime."

Shocked, and somewhat traumatized, I found myself agreeing to things I barely understood, too many thoughts and conflicting emotions going off within me. But the main thought that dominated all others was that for the next two or three weeks, I would be able to breathe normally.

CHAPTER 2
ECHO

I entered one of the private meeting chambers of the spaceport, feeling giddy beyond words. A tall glass wall divided the relatively small room in the middle, keeping the visitors in a pressurized space suited for them. Within, the familiar face of Kayog Voln smiled at me.

It was my second time meeting him. The bird-like humanoid with empathic abilities had something noble and almost majestic about him. He resembled a bird of paradise with maroon wings, golden down feathers over his chest and a long, white, fluffy tail that trailed behind him. He had a small beak and silver eyes that spoke of infinite wisdom.

"Greetings, Master Voln," I said as I approached the bench in front of the small table propped against the glass wall.

"Greetings, Echo," Kayog said, also taking a seat on the bench on his side of the wall. "It is a pleasure to see you again after what I must say has been a long and difficult search."

"Am I that unlikable?" I asked teasingly.

He chuckled and shook his head. "You know that is not the case," he replied playfully.

I knew indeed. Finding compatible brides for us on Triton had always been a challenge, not only because it was a water world, but because most compatible species who are part of the United Planets Organization wouldn't survive in our atmosphere. Sadly, with the Sikarians' low birth rates, which unfortunately skewed towards an excess of males, many of us struggled to find a mate. Therefore, I was beyond excited that the Temern had finally found one for me.

"I am a little curious though as to why you requested a new meeting, not that I mind seeing you," I amended.

He smiled, not offended in the least. "Under normal circumstances, you are correct. Since I already performed your psychic assessment, I would have merely sent you her profile and a vidcom conversation between us would have sufficed to finalize the agreement."

"Which means these circumstances are abnormal," I said with a sliver of worry.

"Indeed, they are," Kayog conceded. "First, you should know that, although she consented to the union and is committed to making it work, Neera was not looking for a mate. Health issues require her to leave Earth or die. All the tests indicate Triton is the ideal environment for her to recover and thrive."

"That sounds like a perfect arrangement," I said, still confused as to the issue. "Whether she was looking for a mate or not shouldn't matter since, in the end, we are bound to be happy as we are a perfect match."

To my shock, Kayog flinched and gave me an apologetic look.

"In this instance, I sadly cannot swear that it is the case. I *believe* you are a perfect match. Unfortunately, when I met Neera on Earth, she was back into the real world and in great physical and mental distress. That affected my ability to properly assess her personality."

"In the real world?" I asked, more baffled than ever.

"Neera is an awakening Thalan. However, her mother's poor choices while she was pregnant with her have greatly tampered with Neera's system," Kayog explained. "Her mutation is stalled. But as her lungs—among other things—have already partially transformed, her world is poisoning her with its high levels of oxygen."

"I see…" I said, my enthusiasm significantly dampened by this news. "But does she have gills? This is, after all, a water world."

Kayog heaved a sigh, and my heart sank a bit more as I waited for him to reply.

"No, she does not. And that is the other issue. You asked me why I came here, it is because I must make sure you know exactly all the risks involved in this union, and for me to assess your response to it."

"You're afraid I will say yes out of desperation but not really mean it?" I asked in a clipped tone.

"No, I'm not worried about that. Reading you can help me understand what your main concerns might be that could prevent this union from happening. People rarely vocalize what truly troubles them, not out of deception, but often because they're not even aware of it," Kayog said in a gentle tone. "I really hope you will give this union a chance, but it must be an enlightened decision."

"There are breathing masks she can use to go underwater, but I suspect there is more," I said, bracing for it.

"Although she's currently stalled, the mutation could trigger again at any moment," Kayog explained. "If and when that happens, it will be vital that you become her mentor and teach her how to master her new body. The five weeks following a human's awakening are crucial in flexing those new organs and muscles. Failure to do so would leave her crippled for life."

"That would not be a problem," I said, rather excited by that prospect. "It would be like a rehearsal for when we have our own offspring. But the look on your face tells me there's still more."

The Temern nodded. "Should Neera go through a full mutation—which could happen in a week, in ten years, or maybe never—there is a chance that the atmosphere of Triton will stop being suitable for her. If she becomes a full Sikarian Thalan, she may be forced to leave and go to your original homeworld of Sikaria."

That knocked the wind out of me. The trouble wasn't just the fact that I could invest myself emotionally in my mate only to see her forced to walk away, but the fact that I could spend years, maybe even decades living in the fear of losing her... of our children losing their mother—should we be so blessed to have them.

"What are the odds that she will go through the full mutation?" I asked.

"According to Meri Atani, the Sikarian doctor who evaluated her, there's a fifty-fifty chance," Kayog replied.

I pursed my lips and gave the Temern a dejected look. "You're not exactly painting an overly appealing picture right now."

He gave me a sympathetic look. "I realize that, but you know I would never blindside you."

"I appreciate it, even though it's not the type of news I

was expecting to receive." I lowered my gaze while pondering his words. "What happens if I refuse her?"

"Then I will continue to search for another potential mate for her or advise Neera that she should consider settling for a loveless match. There are species that are even more challenging to pair than yours and who will take anyone that would have them. Not an ideal solution for Neera, but it would save her life."

I flinched at such a prospect, then studied the features of the matrimonial agent. "Do you really think there is a chance that she and I could be a match?"

"I sincerely do. I simply cannot *swear* to it. Echo, you know how rare it is for one of you to find a compatible and willing mate. As with all marriages organized through the PMA, both partners must commit to trying to make things work for six months at the end of which either or both can decide to end the union if there is no chemistry. I think you have a lot more to gain than to lose by giving this a try."

I nodded, his words echoing the thoughts that were going through my mind. "She knows what I am and what I look like?"

"She does," Kayog confirmed. "Although Neera found your appearance a little strange, which is to be expected, she thought you pleasant to the eye. She's also excited by the fact that you are one of the people she's turning into... or at least might turn into. It makes her feel safer."

I heaved a sigh, already knowing what I would say before the words even formed on my tongue. "Very well, Master Voln. Let's give this a try."

"I have a feeling you will not regret it," the Temern said with the stiff stretching of his beak that served as a beaming smile.

~

I spent the following week learning all that I could about humans, making some adjustments to the beach house for her, and preparing for Neera's arrival. My mother was beside herself with excitement, constantly offering her services to help with this or that, and especially wanting to organize an over-the-top wedding for us. I had to keep reminding her that, as a human, Neera would not be able to take part in an underwater wedding, especially not on the day of her arrival and with her medical condition. Still, it was good to be able to rely on her to handle some of the more administrative aspects of welcoming a landbound, off-worlder bride while I continued learning of her culture and her needs.

My father was still off at sea and would sadly not return in time for the wedding. Under different circumstances, we would have postponed the ceremony until his return. However, the PMA had a number of very strict rules that needed to be observed in order for the union to be considered valid. Straying from any of them could have serious repercussions, including having the marriage considered null and void, with brutal financial penalties for the partner at fault or for both, based on the circumstances that led to such default.

Thankfully, although we celebrated weddings here, they were not a major deal. With such a low female population, very few people actually married during their fertile years, unless they found their true soulmate. Most couples were fairly fluid, and in many cases, a single female would have two or three different partners. My own parents were not married. My father was one of my mother's three main partners. Unfortunately, she had not managed to conceive another child since me. Nevertheless, she held onto hope, considering she was only 51 years old. With our lifespan averaging 180 years, she would still be fertile for another 70 years at least.

And this was the true cause for celebration: pregnancies, especially when it was a female. The thought of having a little girl of my own had my heart filling to bursting.

But first, I needed to make my way to the spaceport to meet my bride in the flesh and have the human wedding to seal that first part of our contract. After one last look at the beach house, I headed out, debating which means of transportation made the most sense to go get Neera. I no sooner stepped outside than I saw my mother making a beeline for me. I didn't know whether I was amused or annoyed. You'd almost think she was the one getting married.

"You're heading out?" my mother asked.

"Yes. Neera's ship should be docking with the space station in the next thirty minutes, with another twenty minutes or so for the shuttle to take her to the spaceport. I want to be there early."

She gave me an approving smile. "Good thinking. It will make your mate feel valued." She cast a glance at the beachside near the darter stables.

Guessing what thoughts were crossing her mind, I preemptively answered. "I was considering fetching her on a darter ray, but I'm not sure if she suffers from motion sickness or is afraid of heights. I also don't know how many personal items she came with. Although less exciting, a shuttle should make her more comfortable and allow us to transport whatever she has with her."

My mother pursed her lips in that adorable way that always made me want to chuckle. I had inherited most of my facial features from her and my father's broad frame and non-negligible height. But, personality-wise, you'd often think I was the parent, and she was my spoiled child.

I flicked her pouty lips with my index finger. "Stop pouting, Mother. I agree that it would make a far more impressive display to show up riding a darter ray, but she won't even be there when I arrive, and I do not want her feeling frightened."

She waved a dismissive hand. "If she is frightened then she will probably wrap her arms around you and bury her face in your chest while hanging on for dear life. It is as good a way as any to create the first bond."

"Mother! Any male who has to resort to having a woman frightened in order for her to embrace him has a serious problem. My female will hold me because she wants me. And she will… Now I have to go. And please behave when I return with Neera. Do not overwhelm her. I know you."

"Getting to know my daughter-in-law and making her feel welcomed hardly qualifies as overwhelming someone," she argued, frowning at me.

"When it comes from you, it definitely qualifies. AND," I added quickly when she opened her mouth to argue, "the one person she needs to get to know first and foremost is yours truly. The first few days of a new relationship are critical. I need you to stay out of my business while I bond with my mate."

"Fine. Be that way."

I chuckled at her grumpy expression, knowing deep down she wasn't actually upset, just very excited. "Love you, Mother. I'll see you soon."

I leaned forward and kissed her forehead. She smiled, caressed my cheek, and nodded with an air of encouragement. Turning around, I made my way to the ship hangar. The off-white sand crunched beneath my bare feet. I loved its warmth and powdery softness, yielding at first when you stepped on it, then growing firm as it held you up. I hoped Neera would appreciate the beauty of Triton and grow to love this planet as much as I did.

A few of the villagers—especially the males—shouted some encouragement, some a little more lurid than others as they watched me head towards the hangar. I picked one of the common personal shuttles shared by the community, settled in, and took flight.

A darter ray would have made for a much grander entrance, but Neera wouldn't have seen it. Vaguely reminiscent of Earth's manta ray, they possessed a double set of fins that also served as wings, a flat, snake-looking head, and a set of horns on their backs that served as handles. Darter ray races, both underwater and in the air, constituted one of the main tourist attractions of Triton.

But even as I began the short twenty-minute journey to the spaceport, I began to wonder if I should have put some clothes on or adorned myself in any way before our first meeting. My people didn't wear clothes, although we had long scarves that could be used as sarongs. We also rarely wore any particular adornments, except pearls and shells in our hair, or as necklaces, and the occasional bioluminescent ink on our bodies. However, they were all usually only worn for special events.

Either way, it's too late to turn back now.

Not that I actually wanted to. In the end, this new relationship needed to have a solid foundations based on honesty. It wouldn't do either of us any good for me to present myself in one way knowing that our everyday reality would be quite different. I just hoped she wouldn't assume it meant I didn't care enough to make myself more attractive to her.

Humans had all kinds of strange preening rituals before meeting with a potential or existing partner—especially females. Aside from the multiple layers of clothes, the women walked in shoes with impossibly high heels that HAD to be painful, encased themselves inside a variety of confining undergarments, painted their faces, lips, and eyes in ways that could radically change their natural appearance, and did elaborate things to their hair, some hairdos requiring hours to complete. And then, they covered themselves in artificial pheromones to further entice their partner.

Their males seemed to have an easier time of it, most not painting their faces, but trimming or removing their facial hair. Some of them also spent a long time fixing their hair, despite it being much shorter. And they, too, splashed artificial pheromones on their bodies.

It boggled my mind that so much of a human's seduction ritual would depend on external items or artificial enhancements, on top of their natural attributes. Very few other species I knew—whether sapient or merely sentient—relied so heavily on factors other than their own genetic assets and skills. I couldn't wait to show Neera mine.

Will she adorn and artificially enhance herself for me?

To my surprise, I felt torn about it. A part of me hoped she would, not only as a display she cared enough to want to please me by looking her best, but also out of curiosity as to what she deemed her most favorable appearance. Then the other hoped she wouldn't. I wanted to see and enjoy her natural beauty and scent. It could also be an indication that she had educated herself about my people as much as I had tried to educate myself about hers—a prospect that pleased me greatly. Then again, maybe it would simply mean she couldn't be bothered. After all, she had not been looking for a mate.

But Kayog says she's determined to make our union work.

With too many thoughts racing through my mind, I finally landed the shuttle outside the spaceport and quickly made my way in. As usual, there was hardly anyone around. We didn't get many visitors aside from trade ships. With our planet being a water world and what was considered a semi hostile environment, few people attempted to illegally come here or sneak in. There were only a couple of guards that also served as customer service for the rare times they were required.

I made a beeline for one of the bigger meeting halls, Hall 14, that I had reserved specifically for the occasion. This room could comfortably accommodate twenty people on each side of the protective wall. To my delight, I had arrived before them, as I had hoped. However, the wait soon proved to be a form of torture in and of itself as I started imagining all the things that could go wrong. I mainly feared she would be less than impressed with me. Naturally, uncertainties about showing up naked reared their heads again.

I tapped the holographic interface on the separation glass to get an idea of the ETA of my mate's ship. My heart leapt in my chest upon seeing it had docked only seconds ago. Feeling incredibly nervous, I ran my fingers through my hair hoping to fix it a little, although it didn't need it, then smoothed the scales of my veil—the pelvic membrane that covered my modesty.

Time slowly went by. I was on the verge of climbing the walls when the back door of the room finally parted. Kayog walked in first, followed by an older human female I didn't know, and then finally my Neera, carrying a bag.

She looked smaller and more fragile than I anticipated, which immediately had every single protective instinct in me surging to the fore. I couldn't tell if her health issues or financial situation were to blame, but my female looked far too skinny. I could already tell my mother would be feeding Neera around the clock until she begged for mercy.

Like most Thalan females, Neera had very long and mostly straight hair down to the middle of her back. It was dark brown, not quite black, with slightly reddish undertones. Her wheatish skin complexion, with its sun-kissed, golden-yellowish color, gave away the Indian origins of at least one of her parents. From a distance, her eyes looked rather dark, but from the images Kayog had sent me, I knew them to be a beautiful golden-green color.

Neera was eyeing me with the same curiosity I felt about her but maintained a neutral enough expression to make it impossible for me to guess what thoughts were crossing her mind. She didn't look turned off or disappointed by my appearance, but she also didn't seem particularly thrilled or impressed.

"Hello, Echo," Kayog said in a joyful voice. "It is good to see you again so soon."

Forcing myself to look away from her, I returned the Temern's warm greeting. "Hello, Master Voln. Ladies..." I added, nodding at each of the two females in turn.

"This is Isobel Biondi, a human priestess affiliated to the United Planets Organization," Kayog explained. "She will officiate your human union. And this is your bride, Neera Michaels. Neera, Isobel, meet Echo Doja, the groom."

"It is a pleasure to meet you, Mr. Doja," the priestess said with a friendly smile.

"The pleasure is all mine," I replied in a similar fashion. I then turned my eyes to my mate, who appeared a little intimidated. "We meet at last, Neera. Welcome to your new home. I hope you will find happiness here with me and your new people."

"Thank you. It certainly is an exciting new adventure."

I instantly liked the sultry sound of her voice and the unexpected firmness of her tone. For some reason, maybe because of her fragile appearance, I had expected a timid whisper.

I nodded. "Most certainly. I have no doubt you will find Triton quite fascinating."

I then cast an inquisitive look at Kayog. He immediately gave me a subtle nod before turning to my mate.

"Unless anyone has further questions, we will now proceed with the union," the Temern said. When the two females expressed their assent, Kayog gestured for Neera to approach the glass wall. "You must join your mate on the other side for the ceremony."

She eyed the glass wall with an uncertain look, obviously not seeing the way through. It was designed so that only natives could activate the hidden door in order for an off-worlder to enter this side of the spaceport, which then gave free access to the whole planet.

I tapped on the glass to call up again the holographic interface that had timed out since I had previously consulted it to see when their ship would arrive. From the menu, I activated the door. A blue light scanned me to confirm I was a Thalan. Then a section of the glass wall, in the shape of a large door, appeared to liquefy, turning in fact into an energy field that anyone could pass through without compromising the integrity of the pressurized room my guests were currently standing in.

Neera's eyes widened in surprise, but then she advanced towards it with determined steps that once more impressed me. Despite knowing how desperate her situation had been on Earth, I had nonetheless expected her to be a bit more skittish now that things were getting real. As soon as she crossed the field, a shiver coursed through her body.

A strong feeling also tugged at me. Whatever doubts or uncertainties any of us had as far as Neera's future here on Triton or with me, there was no question she was a Sikarian. Our people, regardless of the breed they belong to, always felt an instant connection when in the presence of another of our kin. Neera was one of us trapped in a human body.

However, the way she looked around the room made me wonder if she had felt the Sikarian connection or if the shift in pressure had triggered that shiver. My mate put down her bag, carefully removed her mask, and took in a few timid breaths, the tension in her body betraying her fear that it might reject this atmosphere. The redness on her face where her mask had applied pressure on her skin upset me. I didn't need to ask to know the skin was tender, and that it had hurt her to wear it.

Neera suddenly took on an embarrassed expression and two of her fingers lightly brushed over the red bruises. Her reaction took me aback for a moment. Then I realized my face must have betrayed my displeasure, and she misinterpreted my expression.

"I'm sorry you have been forced to endure such discomfort for the simple right to breathe," I quickly said to clarify where I was coming from. "It warms my heart to know that you will no longer have to endure such pain again in the future."

With each word, tension drained from her shoulders, and she gave me a grateful smile.

"Being rid of this couldn't come soon enough," she said with a sheepish grin. "But even as uncomfortable as it has been, I cannot hate this mask. It has quite literally saved my life this whole time."

I nodded and gestured for her to come closer. She immediately complied and came to stand barely a meter in front of me. I loved her height. With my 6'5, I towered over her by a good head. I estimated her to be around 5'8, the perfect height to bury her face in my neck when we would embrace.

Neera had kept her adornments to a minimum. A dark line creating a wing on her top eyelids, a thickener on her natural eyelashes, and a pale gloss on her lips appeared to be the only facial enhancements she had given herself. Small teardrop pearl earrings dangled from her earlobes, a simple sleeveless white dress hid nothing of the shape of her body, and a delicate spicy scent emanated from her. It pleased me as my mate had followed her people's custom of adorning themselves while keeping it minimalistic enough that she remained her true self, not some deceptively painted doll.

The priestess approached the glass. "As per the instructions given to me, we are going to perform an abbreviated human marriage ceremony. If you are both ready to proceed, I would ask you to come closer still and hold both of each other's hands."

We complied, both of us each taking a step forward. An odd thrill coursed through me when Neera placed her delicate hands in mine. They were soft and warm, and held me with a very pleasant firmness devoid of any trembling. It pleased me to no end that she wasn't being skittish or showing any type of regrets or second thoughts at having accepted me. I smiled. She held my gaze unflinchingly and responded in kind.

"We are gathered here to celebrate the union of this woman, Neera Michaels, and this Sikarian male, Echo Doja, in the sacred bond of marriage. Such union must be entered into with honest intentions, deep commitment, and not for financial gains or deceptive purposes. Neera Michaels, do you freely take this Sikarian male, Echo Doja, to be your lawfully wedded husband, for better or for worse, through good times and hardships, in sickness and in health, until death do you part?"

"I do," Neera said without hesitation.

"Echo Doja, do you freely take this woman, Neera Michaels, to be your lawfully wedded wife, for better or for worse, through good times and hardships, in sickness and in health, until death do you part?"

"I do," I replied.

"Kayog Voln, do you confirm that you bore witness to this human female, Neera Michaels, and this Tritonian male, Echo Doja, freely committing to be legally married to each other in accordance with the human and galactic laws?"

"I do confirm it," Kayog said.

"By the power vested in me by the Clerical College of Earth and the United Planets Organization, I declare you husband and wife. Echo Doja, you may kiss the bride," the priestess said.

Neera's hands tightened around mine ever so slightly, but I perceived no fear from her expression or body language. I believed nervousness had prompted that reaction. More importantly, she didn't appear repulsed by that prospect. I leaned forward, and she lifted her face towards mine, even rising to her tiptoes until our lips met. Her gaze never wavered from mine the whole duration of the kiss. I could tell she was assessing my reactions the same way I was hers. After a few seconds, I broke the kiss and straightened under the applause of both the priestess and Kayog.

I didn't know what to make of that experience. It foreshadowed a rather interesting wedding night. We turned to face Priestess Biondi and Master Voln. But it was the expression on the Temern's face that held my attention. The way his silver eyes flicked between my mate and me made me suspect he was wondering if our pairing had been a mistake. His empathic abilities likely picked up my suspicions as his expression immediately changed to something more jovial.

I had no doubt the cold and clinical way in which Neera and I kissed had triggered that worry. And yet, for some inexplicable reason, I didn't feel any concern. If my hunch was right, my mate was as analytical as I was, and would likely keep her guard up as she assessed my personality while we defined our relationship together.

The priestess tapped a few instructions on her datapad, which projected the marriage contract onto the interface of the glass wall for Neera and me to sign. We proceeded by pressing our thumbs in our respective signature boxes before Kayog did the same with his.

"All of Neera's belongings are currently being unloaded from the vessel. The shuttle should bring them shortly back to your village," Kayog explained. "As per the agreement, you are expected to perform the Sikarian wedding ritual by nightfall for the contract to be legal. You also have the list of all other conditions that must be honored over the six-month trial period."

"This ceremony will take place tonight," I confirmed. "We have adapted it to account for my mate's anatomy."

Neera gave me a questioning look.

"We normally marry underwater," I explained. "It would be fairly awkward for you, especially since you would be unable to communicate the way we do."

"Right," she said, looking slightly embarrassed. "Thank you for your foresight."

"Of course," I replied, unable to hide my delight at having pleased her.

"Perfect," Kayog said in an approving tone. "Dr. Meri Atani should have transferred all the medical data concerning Neera and awakening Thalans to your head healer. Should there be any changes that would require my assistance, do not hesitate to contact me."

I hated the underlying meaning of his words, but it was still good to know that my mate would be provided for should she be unable to remain here.

"Thank you, Master Voln. Thanks for everything you've done for me," Neera said with a depth of emotions in her voice that moved me.

"Glad to have been of assistance, my dear Neera. I wish the two of you great happiness in your union."

After exchanging a few more pleasantries, we finally said our goodbyes and went our separate ways. I picked up Neera's bag before leading her towards the exit. Her eyes were flicking this way and that, taking in her environment with a healthy level of curiosity and awe. That pleased me tremendously.

"Have you ever been off-world before?" I asked as I led her out of the building.

She shook her head, her steps faltering as she cast a first

glance at our colorful sky, with its shades of pink, blue, and purple. She inhaled deeply, a radiant expression descending on her rather attractive features. She turned her golden-green eyes towards me and beamed at me.

"I think I'm going to love it here," Neera said in a voice filled with emotion.

"I will make sure you do, my mate."

CHAPTER 3
NEERA

E cho was far taller and bigger than I had thought. He was also far more attractive in person than his holographic image had hinted. I never thought a guy with pinkish skin, pink scales, and red hair could look so manly and virile. Yeah... it had been narrow-minded of me. Keeping my eyes to myself was proving to be quite the challenge.

As expected, my brand-new husband was strutting about completely naked. Granted, the scales partially acted as cover for his nudity, but they hid nothing of the muscular shapes and curves of his body. Thankfully, just like my research had indicated, Thalans possessed a veil: flowy, scale-covered hip fins that wrapped around their pelvis to form some kind of short Roman skirt to hide their naughty bits and butt cracks. When opened, the fins could either hang loosely on the sides of their thighs or flatten against their bodies in an almost seamless pattern.

Beautiful pink and white opal-colored scales, forming an exquisite but very discreet undulating pattern covered Echo's veil. Although human in appearance, his hands and feet were webbed. From my reading, I'd found out that vicious claws could extrude from both sets of nails, and that the bones of his heels and ankles—the talus and calcaneus—would shift positions when he formed his 'tail' to swim. I couldn't wait to witness that.

"I came to get you in a shuttle. I didn't know how many things you would be carrying or if you were afraid of heights. Otherwise, I would have brought a darter ray," Echo said in that very enticingly throaty voice of his.

He had a very subtle accent when he spoke Universal that I couldn't quite define and was failing to find any other to compare it to. It was nonetheless quite pleasant, especially for me, who was a sucker for deep voices.

I made no effort to hide my sad face. "That was very thoughtful of you, but also unfortunate. I am not afraid of heights, and I won't lie that I'm quite looking forward to riding one of those creatures," I said sheepishly. "I've been reading a lot about your world... at least all that I could get my hands on. It sounds quite fascinating. I'm really excited at the prospect of experiencing it all."

"Your words have not fallen on deaf ears, Neera. Soon, you will be begging me for a reprieve," Echo said with a mischievous grin. "This world is immense, and our underwater world even more so."

"Do your worst," I challenged with a grin of my own. "Chances are, I'll be the one wearing you out first."

He laughed, his very pale eyes gleaming with mirth. "Challenge accepted, my mate," he said in a friendly tone.

I loved the sound of his laughter; deep, rumbling, and with that same sexy throatiness as when he spoke. It made him quite attractive. As strange as some of his features were to me, I had to admit that my husband was a rather handsome male.

Considering that one of the provisions in the Prime Mating Agency's contract required the newlyweds to consummate their marriage on the first night, this was rather good news for me. It would still be super awkward to lie with someone I'd just met, but unless he turned into a complete freak, I could see myself getting turned on by him.

But will he get turned on by me?

And that was the big question. The way he had checked me out when I first walked into that pressurized room had not gone unnoticed. Unfortunately, he had done too good of a job hiding his thoughts. Was he disappointed by my appearance in the flesh? Going by our wedding kiss, I got the impression he would have taken far more pleasure kissing a sex bot than he did kissing me.

Then again, he probably thought the same about how little enthusiasm I'd displayed myself. I hadn't meant to be so cold. I'd just been too damn focused on assessing his reaction. Me and my damn analytical mind. I couldn't risk alienating him. I needed Echo to more than just like me, but to actually fall in love with me and want to keep me forever. My body—and my lungs—loved this planet, at least so far. I was clearly made for it.

Echo indicated his shuttle, parked near the entrance. Compared to Earth's spaceport, this place looked like a ghost town. I could only see four other shuttles parked nearby. They all had a similar shape, almost like a donut without a hole and a triangular fin on each side.

As soon as we entered the vessel, Echo pointed me to the passenger seat while securing my bag in an overhead compartment. He then settled next to me in the pilot's seat. Seconds later, we were airborne.

We weren't flying high, maybe fifty meters aboveground.

But flying higher would have been pointless as there were no obstacles in sight. To my surprise, after barely five hundred meters, the land gave way to an ocean.

"Whoa, that ended rather abruptly," I said, a little stunned.

Echo chuckled. "Because it isn't natural land. We have very little of that on Triton. The spaceport is one of the many artificial islands or floating cities we have built on this planet. However, our village, Soigo Reef, is a natural formation."

"So, all your houses are on the ground? Not underwater? What I read was rather confusing on that front," I said in an apologetic tone.

He smiled gently. "We have both. Every village or city has open air dwellings and sunken cities. We divide our time equally between the two, although the fingerlings spend most of their time underwater. They only come to the surface for an hour every other day to soak up the sun and experience natural gravity. Once they become juveniles, our young start spending a more equal amount of time between both settings."

"Oh wow, I can't wait to see it all," I said, excitement bubbling in my voice.

Visibly pleased by my enthusiasm, Echo's smile broadened.

He cast an inquisitive look my way. "How tired do you feel right now? It was a long journey from Earth. Do you need rest? Are you hungry? Were the accommodations decent?"

"I'm fine, thank you for asking. The accommodations were quite amazing, to be honest. Kayog had a room especially pressurized for me so that I would be comfortable to sleep or take refuge in when breathing in that mask within the common areas became too difficult."

An approving expression settled on his face. "Excellent.

Kayog is a good male. I knew he would take good care of you."

"He's the best. He thinks of everything," I said, my throat tightening. I immediately felt silly over it. "I'm sorry for getting emotional. But I've never had anyone go out of their way for me like he did. We're perfect strangers, and he owes me nothing. I'm not used to being pampered or looked after like this."

"Well, get used to it, Neera, because that's going to be my duty moving forward," he said matter-of-factly.

"You don't have to do that," I said, scrunching my face.

He gave me an amused sideways glance as if I'd said something cute. "When we reach Soigo, I will introduce you to Rana, our Matriarch, and to my mother, Edlyn. Mother can be a handful in her enthusiasm. Do not hesitate to tell her to slow down if you start feeling overwhelmed. She will not take offense."

"All right," I said, immediately intrigued by the female.

Under different circumstances, his words would have concerned me. However, the amused and affectionate way he'd said it made me think his mother was just the typical colorful but harmless relative everyone shook their heads at but absolutely adored, nonetheless.

"I will then give you a tour of the house. As the day is already quite advanced, my mother will come prepare you for the ceremony. There will first be the binding ritual, the feast, and then the dance."

"The dance?" I repeated, worry filling my voice. "I couldn't find anything on Sikarian weddings."

"Do not worry. It is normally a seduction dance that the couple performs with each other underwater, while surrounded by other dancers, spurring them on," he explained in a soothing voice. "I have adapted the ceremony so that you won't have to dance. Instead, you'll get to sit back and—hopefully—enjoy the show while I attempt to seduce you with my sexiest moves."

I burst out laughing at the exaggerated Casanova face he made while speaking those words. He chuckled in turn, pleased by my reaction.

"Hmm, you drive a hard bargain. Sit back and relax while watching a sexy man bust a move for me? I can think of worse fates," I replied teasingly.

"Ah! So you find me sexy, do you? Then again, how could you not?"

I gasped, and my jaw dropped at the unexpected comment. It was his turn to burst out laughing while heat crept up my cheeks. I realized then he'd said it to elicit specifically this reaction from me.

A sense of humor? I approve.

I hesitated for a second, then decided to respond in kind. "Well, you do have a body that would have any male fitness model on Earth go green with envy. Therefore, I would either have to be dead or blind not to find you sexy."

I expected a smug grin to stretch his rather plush lips. Instead, a colorful wave—mainly of dark reds—flitted over his skin before it abruptly returned to normal. I recoiled, startled by the phenomenon.

"What… what was that?" I asked in an uncertain tone.

Echo shifted in his seat, looking somewhat sheepish. "It is something our bodies sometimes do… when we are embarrassed."

"Oh, my God! Did you just blush?" I exclaimed.

This time, the phenomenon repeated itself but with far

more intensity. I couldn't help laughing again. He looked so incredibly adorable the way he scrunched his face.

"I'm sorry. I didn't mean to embarrass you. I was only teasing—although your fitness level *truly is* phenomenal," I amended. "But this is really cool. Is it your scales changing colors?"

He shook his head with an almost timid smile. "It is my skin doing this. We have bioluminescent skin cells. We can control them to change our color for camouflage, for courtship displays, or to hypnotize prey. To a certain extent, we can even mold our tissue to resemble the texture of an object or of the background we're mimicking. But when we get embarrassed, the cells just kick in on their own. The upside is that we can silence them right away."

"Ah! That's why it stopped so abruptly the first time," I said with sudden understanding.

He nodded. "You will get to see how we use it in an artistic fashion during our wedding ceremony later tonight."

"That sounds great. I'm looking forward to it," I said with a grin.

But even as I spoke those words, another thought that had been poking me for a while crossed my mind again. I gave him a sideways glance and chewed my bottom lip while pondering whether or not to ask it.

"What? Something's troubling you. You can ask me anything, even if it is embarrassing. I want you to feel at home and very comfortable here with us," Echo said in an encouraging tone.

"Thank you, that's very sweet of you. And yes, I have a billion different questions, many of which are definitely of the embarrassing kind. But I'm not quite sure how to qualify this one."

"Ask and we'll see," he said gently.

I cleared my throat and nodded. "It's just... I'm wondering what your people think about a human coming to settle among you. Do they have certain concerns about our marriage?"

"Oh no! Quite the opposite. Every single male—and there are plenty on Triton—is quite envious of me. Everyone was ecstatic to hear that one of us had finally found a match. Even more so finding out that you are our distant kin. As Kayog probably told you, we have a low birth rate in general, and especially few females. It is a blessing for me that Kayog should have deemed me a good match for you and an even greater one that you have accepted me. My people—*your* new people—are looking forward to meeting you and all rejoice at my good fortune."

The sincerity of his tone and of his expression as he spoke lifted the weight that had been sitting on my shoulders from the moment I had accepted this union. Adapting to a new world, a new species, and a completely alien culture was already a lot to tackle. Not having to battle the rejection of his people was definitely a huge relief.

"There," Echo said, pointing at a quickly growing structure in the distance. "This is Soigo. We will be there in a couple more minutes."

My eyes widened as the island grew bigger on the horizon. At first, I could only see a small mountain range covered in greenery and exotic trees. Then they gave way to a large valley with some crops and lots of one-story houses. A couple of larger buildings looked like they served as a ship hangar and warehouse. The architecture vaguely reminded me of the Hindu Kalinga style, but with less projections along the roofs and walls. Their slightly rounded edges gave the structures a lovely organic feel. From what I had read, they were built out of clay bricks in the paler spectrum of the earthy pastel color palette.

Most of the houses lined the beach area of the bay. In a large, open section in the center of the beach—which could have easily served as the town square—a long, rectangular, stone fire table appeared to serve as a grill. All around it, a number of circular tables were being set by countless people. I realized then that they were preparing the banquet for our upcoming nuptials. My stomach fluttered as the shuttle began its descent.

"Do you have any food allergies?" Echo asked, noticing what had retained my attention.

I shook my head. "I do not have any known allergies. However, I am mostly a pescatarian. I don't have anything against meat, but I never really took to it."

Echo grinned in response. "Good! While some of us do eat meat, it ranks very low in our diet. We mostly eat fish, both cooked and raw, mollusks and crustaceans, various plants and seaweed, fruits and nuts, and some grains and vegetables that we grow on land. You will get to sample many of the dishes tonight."

"I admit that I am quite curious to try your version of sushi, and especially to taste your cooked dishes. There wasn't much information about it online."

"Hopefully, you will find many things to your liking. While we will not be able to accommodate you with certain Earth ingredients and produce, there are certain things that we should be able to order for you should you truly crave them."

I smiled gratefully at him. "To be honest, I'm not really difficult. Probably the one thing I will miss the most are spices. But I'm definitely open to discovering new things."

"Spices are the easiest thing we can have delivered here for you," he replied smugly.

As he spoke those words, he initiated the landing. A few of the people below waved at us as our shuttle headed for one of the two large buildings I had correctly assumed to be a ship hangar.

My stomach knotted with resurging apprehension at how I would be welcomed. Although Echo was so far proving to be rather pleasant, there was an undeniable shyness and awkwardness between us. We'd so far kept to pretty neutral topics, but what were you really supposed to say to someone you'd only met for the first time thirty minutes ago and gotten married to within five minutes of that first meeting?

Echo landed the shuttle with impressive dexterity in the hangar. For some silly reason, I didn't expect merfolk to be this comfortable with landlubber technology and devices. Then again, the Sikarians were one of the most advanced races in the known galaxy, having settled and terraformed a great deal of worlds over millions of years. Granted the Tritonians were settlers that had evolved on a slightly different path than the original people of their homeworld. However, they still remained in close contact and continued to exchange relevant technology that kept Triton from being considered a primitive planet.

In many ways, it could be deemed that Kayog had cheated by using the Prime Mating Agency's program to fund my relocation here. But the reproductive issues of the locals and the fact that they did not pursue interstellar travel more or less made them qualify for the prerequisites of the program. Either way, I was grateful.

I unbuckled my seatbelt with slightly shaky hands. Echo noticed and gave me a sympathetic look.

"I will not pretend to know how you must feel right now," he said in a gentle voice. "It must be stressful to meet so many strangers on a foreign planet you are now supposed to call home. But do not trouble yourself. Your presence here is both welcome and wanted. If you feel overwhelmed at any point in time, you only have to say so, and I will take you somewhere private where you can gather yourself. No one will take offense or think ill of you for it. Do you understand?"

I nodded, my throat tightening with emotion.

"Then promise me you will speak up if you feel uncomfortable," he insisted in a firm voice.

"I promise," I said, feeling inexplicably relieved.

"Good girl! Now, let's introduce you to the villagers."

He picked up my bag and gestured for me to follow him as he exited the shuttle. Even as we walked down the ramp, a couple of people inside the hangar waved at us. For a moment, I thought Echo was going to stop and do formal introductions. When he didn't, I wondered how to interpret it. Instead, we left the building and walked through the streets mostly made of packed dirt, although a handful were covered in stone tiles. We passed many people, all of them waving at us—or more specifically at me—with welcoming smiles, but none approached to strike up a conversation.

I cast a sideways glance at Echo, only to see he was studying my reaction. For some strange reason, my face heated.

"There are too many people for me to start overwhelming you with all of their names. Unless humans have a much greater memory than ours, I doubt you will recall more than five or six names today. Therefore, I will only formally introduce you to the most important people for you to know right now. The others, you can grow to know over the upcoming weeks and months," Echo explained in a gentle tone. "Everyone already knows your name and who you are. They know not to overwhelm you and will not take offense if you forget or mix up their names for a while."

I gave him a sheepish grin, gratitude flooding through me. "Thank you. I am horrible with names. I have an excellent memory when it comes to face recognition, but names are a whole different ball game."

"Well then, for today, focus on remembering three names: mine, my mother Edlyn, and our Matriarch Rana."

"Let's see... The Matriarch Rana, your mother Edlyn, and... hmm... What's your name again?"

His approving nod as I mentioned the first two names instantly vanished, and he gaped at me with a shocked expression. I burst out laughing, my mischievous expression giving away the fact that I was pulling his leg.

"Echo, of course I remember your name," I said teasingly.

His expression softened, but judging by the look on his face, and especially that unreadable smile, I immediately sensed that he would get even at some point.

I liked that...

As we cleared a large tree with beautifully exotic flowers dangling from its vines, whatever else I wanted to say died in my throat. The wide beach crowded with people opened up before us. Every single eye turned to watch us approach. I'd never felt more intimidated, self-conscious... or lacking.

CHAPTER 4
NEERA

The Thalans of Triton were beautiful. They looked slightly different than the ones from their homeworld, Sikaria. Just like their buildings, they came in various shades of pastel colors, but this time not limited to earth tones. Like Echo, each individual's skin, scales, and hair were a variation of a unique color. Every single one of them had bodies to die for.

The women, all bare chested, had boobs so damn perky it should be deemed illegal. Their narrow waists, flaring hips, and endless legs gave the term having an hourglass figure a whole new meaning. Their long hair, down to their middle or lower backs seemed to point to the perfectly round globes of their behinds. Not that the males had anything to be embarrassed about when it came to grabbable butts. Every last male looked like a fitness model, but not bulky like bodybuilders. They had a swimmer's body but with more defined abs and biceps.

A superb female appearing to be in her mid-forties strutted her way towards me. She had sandy skin—a shade slightly paler than mine—and tan scales with golden undertones. With her amber eyes and golden blond hair, she made a striking figure. There was something regal about her, and I instinctively knew she had to be the Matriarch. Next to her—although more like a step behind her—another stunning female was approaching. She appeared to be of an age with me, mid-to-late twenties.

Her dark purple hair and violet eyes contrasted nicely with her pale lilac-colored skin and scales. Where the older female had a calm serenity about her, this one seemed to bubble with excitement. Echo eyeing the second female with a sliver of worry instantly had all of my senses on high alert. She intensely stared at me, but as they reached us, instead of stopping a meter or so in front of us, she went to stand next to Echo. She caressed his shoulder, her hand resting on his upper arm in an affectionate and possessive way that screamed familiarity.

The instant "What the fuck?!" that went off in my mind didn't have time to fully express itself as Echo started talking.

"Matriarch, it is my honor to introduce you to my mate, Neera Michaels. Neera, please meet the Matriarch of Soigo Reef, Rana Ajira."

"It is a pleasure to meet you, Neera of Earth," the Matriarch said in a musical voice that was both soothing and enchanting.

"The honor is all mine, Matriarch," I said with deference while trying to keep my eyes on her instead of on the female touching my husband.

Echo slipped an arm around the waist of the beautiful younger female and pushed her a little forward towards me. "Mother, this is my mate, Neera. Neera, meet my mother, Edlyn Doja."

"Your mother?!" The words burst out of my mouth as I watched the young beauty with my eyes all but popping out of my head. "But... but... Wow, you look stunning. You look like you could be his girlfriend or baby sister."

The words no sooner spilled out than I flinched inwardly, wanting to kick myself. It wasn't like me to speak out of turn. To my relief, all three burst out laughing.

"Well, thank you, daughter. I welcome the compliment," Edlyn said with a grin. "Considering how often he chastises me, Echo would likely tell you that he indeed feels like my big brother rather than my son."

"Truer words were never spoken," Echo said with pretend discouragement.

To my surprise, Edlyn pulled away from her son and came to stand directly in front of me. She cupped my face in her hands with a gentleness that messed me up inside.

"Today is a blessed day that my only son should have found a mate. Welcome to your new home, Neera. It is my hope that, in time, you will grow to consider me as a friend and a mother. If you ever have any questions or need anything, my door will always be open to you."

My throat tightened with emotion. To think I had been so worried about the type of welcome I would receive here. Growing up as an orphan, shuffled around from one foster home to another, I'd never known the love and support of a mother. Sure, my caretakers had been good and decent people. However, to them, I had just been another charge to take care of, a duty, and a source of income. No words could describe how desperately I hungered for a family and a true sense of belonging.

"Thank you, Mrs. Doja. This means the world to me," I said with gratitude.

She waved a dismissive hand and made a face as if I'd said something offensive. "Pfft, Mrs. Doja? I'll have none of that. You may call me Edlyn, Mother, or Trouble, as my irreverent son loves to call me."

Echo chuckled, his face showing no remorse whatsoever, while I gave him a disbelieving sideways glance.

He shrugged with a grin. "I will not try to justify anything. You will understand soon enough."

"Do not let your mate fool you, Neera," the Matriarch said in a mysterious voice. "Edlyn is only trouble in the best kind of way. But we have hogged you enough for now. We will let Echo take you home and give you a chance to settle in before Edlyn comes to prepare you for the wedding. I'm afraid that only gives you thirty minutes or so."

"That's not a problem," I said reassuringly, despite the nervous jolt that coursed through me.

"Excellent. We will see you again shortly," Rana said.

"See you soon," Edlyn repeated.

With a gentle pressure on the small of my back, Echo nudged me forward as we made our way towards a group of houses on the eastern side of the bay. To my pleasant surprise, he took me to a house that had a stunning view directly on the beach. Like all the other dwellings, his didn't have a garden, a backyard, a front terrace or patio. I loved the slightly curved shape of the roof which reminded me of an Indian temple. Despite the simpler patterns adorning it, the work was nonetheless exquisite. I then realized that the front corners of the dwelling were in fact sculptures depicting what vaguely resembled an alien seahorse rising out of a coral reef and pointing its head towards the heavens. Their heads stopped right before the roof.

We climbed the three short steps to the entrance, and the

door automatically parted in front of us. But a surprised yelp escaped me when I felt a strong suction beneath me. It lasted no more than a second or two, with the type of sound a vacuum makes when it sucks in something that gets stuck. I jumped back and cast a frightened look at the narrow porch.

Echo chuckled before giving me an apologetic look. "Do not be scared, Neera. I should have warned you that every residence has a vacuum at the entrance. As you can see, we walk around barefoot in the sand. Our houses would constantly be messy with us going in and out. The vacuum rids us of sand and of any excess moisture that might still be clinging to us if we just came out of the water."

"Right," I said, glaring at the barely visible openings on the porch.

Echo gestured for me to come. I complied, my heart still leaping a little when I stepped back onto the porch and the suction occurred again. But walking into the house quickly wiped away all thoughts of that scare. I didn't really know what I had expected his house would look like, but certainly not for it to be this colorful without being overly loud or tacky.

Clearly, he had attempted to give the interior an under-water feeling without going all out to make it into an actual aquarium. The walls were painted a light blue color and the furniture all had a design inspired by conches, shells, corals, or undersea creatures. It wasn't literal, but certain shapes or patterns clearly hinted at the original source. Colorful cushions and throw pillows gave the seating area the same type of color palette one would find around a coral reef.

The kitchen surprised me in that there were very few cupboards, a fairly small cooling unit, but a very sexy cooking plate, complete with grill. Next to the cooling unit sat a large glass tank with a fancy interface. Although filled with water, it didn't contain anything.

"Our people eat fresh every day," Echo explained when he caught me eyeing the tank. "We either catch our own seafood in the morning or go buy some from the fishermen and put them in a reservoir until we are ready to consume them. In our floating cities, the reservoirs are actually connected to the holding tanks. There, you only have to select the seafood you want from the interface, and it will be sent directly into your tank."

"That sounds pretty sweet," I said, impressed.

He shrugged. "It is. But I prefer catching my own. Come, let me show you the rest of the house."

There were only four other rooms: the master bedroom, the guest room—which he was hoping would one day become a child's bedroom—the hygiene room, although merely toilet, was more accurate, and a workroom. Naturally, as they didn't wear any clothes, there were no laundry rooms or wardrobes.

"Well, I am relieved to see you have normal toilets—by human standards—I'm a little surprised you don't have showers. Do you not rinse off the salt water from your bodies?" I asked.

"Actually, Soigo is surrounded by freshwater. But to answer your question, we don't have to, even though we often do. We go to the freshwater waterfall to rinse off," he replied.

"I see," I said, realizing how awkward it would likely be for me at first.

He gestured for me to enter the master bedroom. It was an average sized room, with wide windows. A king size bed ate up a large section of the room. I didn't quite know how to describe its shape: neither rectangular nor oval. But the headboard definitely resembled a shell. The night stands on each side of the bed reminded me of a wave rising out of the sides of the headboard. Here too, there were no wardrobes, only a large display case with a glass cover that showed a series of jewelry. I recognized them as being mostly hair adornments, a few necklaces, and arm bracelets. Next to it sat a small chest of drawers.

"Did you bring a lot of clothes?" Echo asked with a strange expression.

I had wondered when that topic would be brought up. I swallowed hard and shook my head. "No. Very little. Mostly undies, a few skirts, and footwear."

His relieved expression and the approving glimmer in his eyes confirmed what I had suspected even before my arrival.

"As you have certainly noticed, my people do not wear clothes," Echo said carefully. "No one will demand that you walk around naked if it is uncomfortable for you."

"But you would prefer I did," I concluded for him.

He shifted uneasily on his feet. "You do not have a veil to cover your pelvic area like we do. It would therefore make sense for you to wear a sarong or something similar. As your feet are soft and do not possess the natural protections we do, it would also be advisable for you to wear sandals or any other footwear that would avoid injuries. Aside from that, you would ideally not wear anything else."

"So, no bra, no top," I said.

He nodded. "Again, if it is too uncomfortable for you, no one will think ill of you for wearing clothes. However, I think that living as we do as much as possible would help your integration. But I will respect your decision either way."

I cleared my throat and nervously scratched my nape while trying to figure out how to word my answer. "I have been mentally preparing for that on my way here. But I have to admit, I didn't expect your people to look so damn perfect. I will feel quite self-conscious for a while. My body certainly cannot compete with that of your women."

He frowned and gave me a slightly baffled look. "Why would you even want or try to compete? You are human, we are Tritonian Thalans. You have no one to impress. And even if you did want to impress someone here, you would never achieve that by showing off your curves. We inherit the body we're born in. Its flawlessness or lack thereof is merely due to the DNA lottery. And even then, as humans say: beauty is in the eye of the beholder. It's who you are, not what you look like that will determine your popularity here. So, please do not fret about such superficial things."

I gave him a sheepish smile. "My head knows that, but my insecurities take a little longer to catch up."

"Then tell your insecurities to get lost," he said with pretend severity. "As long as your body is healthy, the rest is irrelevant. Oxygen poisoning has made you lose a bit too much weight back on Earth. Now that you are in the right environment for you to thrive, we will get you back to your ideal weight. But as for its shape, your body is what it was meant to be. And I, for one, find it pleasant to the eye."

My face heated at the compliment. I couldn't tell if he truly meant it or if he was merely trying to make me feel better about myself. Either way, mission accomplished.

He pointed at the chest of drawers. "This is for you to put your personal belongings in. Let me know if you need something bigger. The two bottom drawers have been set up specifically for you to put your shoes in. In the top drawer, my mother has already placed a dozen scarfs for you to use as sarongs, if you so wish."

"Okay, thank you."

He smiled, then an awkward silence settled between us. It was absurd, considering that as complete strangers, we should have a billion questions about each other that we would want answered. And yet, we both just stood there staring, hoping the other would come up with something to say.

This time, it was his turn to clear his throat. "My mother will be here shortly to prepare you."

"Yeah, the Matriarch mentioned that earlier. What exactly does that mean?"

"It's nothing big. She's only going to help you put on the sarong in a way that is comfortable for you, and then adorn your skin and your hair according to our traditions. It shouldn't take very long," Echo said in a reassuring tone. "When you're done, she will take you to the banquet."

Right on cue, a soft chime resonated through the house. Echo smiled.

"I believe my mother is growing impatient. Hold on."

I watched him leave the room, feeling both relieved and anxious. Echo seemed like a charming man, and he definitely was hot. Unfortunately, I didn't feel the chemistry or connection I had hoped for. If I had been the one-night stand kind of girl, I would have been all in with someone looking like him. But we were talking about marriage, a lifetime commitment. One I absolutely needed to make work, if only for my health.

I could only hope that I was overthinking things. You didn't have to hit it off right away with someone to eventually develop a deep and strong relationship with them. With luck, the awkward uneasiness that had settled between us was just due to our unusual circumstances.

Maybe his mother can help me figure out how to connect with him.

Speaking of the devil, Echo and his mother entered the bedroom where I still stood, my hands clasped before me.

"There she is," Edlyn said with a sweet smile that instantly put me at ease. "Off you go, my sweet. Your mate is in good hands."

Echo nodded in response to his mother, gave me an encouraging smile, then left the room.

Edlyn approached me with determined steps. She was holding two ornate wooden boxes in her hands. A detailed carving of a 3D octopus, its tentacles wrapping around the edges adorned one of the boxes, while the other appeared to have shells and coral reefs sculpted in bas-relief on it. She put them down on top of the chest of drawers before giving me an assessing look.

"Before we start, I have to ask. Did Echo discuss clothes with you?" Edlyn asked.

I nodded, my stomach knotting a little. "Yes, he has. But I already knew I would have to shed my clothes once I moved here."

Edlyn frowned. "You don't *have* to remove your clothes if it makes you uncomfortable. I believe it would be better for your integration, but it's perfectly fine if you need more time to make that transition or if you never do. No one will feel offended if you choose to remain dressed. But as we spend a lot of time in the water, you might want to opt for swimwear instead of traditional human clothes."

Although Echo had said something similar earlier, hearing it from her made me feel even better about it, not that it actually mattered in the end.

"Thank you. I really appreciate how you're all trying to make me feel comfortable here. However, when I came to Triton, I committed to try and adapt to the ways of my new people. Yes, it's going to be super awkward at first, but I'd rather just take the dive and follow your customs right away. Dragging things on forever might just make it harder down the road."

Edlyn smiled, clearly pleased by my answer. "I think it is a wise approach. And that awkwardness will fade sooner than you think. You'll be self-conscious about it because it will be front and center on your mind when you walk out of this dwelling. But after a few minutes of interacting with the others, you will soon get too caught up with everything else to even remember that you are naked. And when you end up remembering, you'll see that it's truly no big deal and that no one cares."

I nodded with a grateful smile. "Your words are logical, but you know how the mind works…"

She chuckled and nodded with sympathy. "The mind certainly has a will of its own. Now, please remove all your clothes, and let's find the perfect sarong for you."

She immediately turned to the chest of drawers and pulled out the neatly folded stacks of sarong scarfs she previously brought in for me. While she did, I proceeded to remove my clothes, repeating in my mind that this was no different than stripping in front of a medical doctor. After taking off my dress and bra, I hesitated about getting rid of my panties.

Fuck it. I said I'd dive. Let's dive.

Just as I started pulling them down, Edlyn picked a couple of scarves, holding them up in front of me, likely to see which one complimented my complexion the most. As I straightened and tossed my panties on top of my dress, I braced for a judgmental once over that never came. My mother-in-law cast a distracted glance at my naked body then turned her attention back to the scarves, mumbling to herself. In that instant, I realized nudity truly meant nothing to them. My human upbringing was making a big deal out of nothing.

"That yellow one is kind of nice," I said timidly, pointing at the golden, embroidered fabric in her hand.

Edlyn looked at it and pursed her lips. "It is nice and looks gorgeous against your light brown skin," she conceded. "But then every color matches your beautiful complexion. The question is which one is the perfect one for this event?"

"Well, traditional Hindu weddings usually have outfits in shades of red, green, yellow, or pink," I offered. "Although I do not follow that religion, I still observe a number of practices of the Indian culture. Since Echo's skin and scales are pink, maybe that shade would make sense?"

"Of course!" Edlyn exclaimed. "It's such an obvious choice. I should have thought of it!"

She pulled out a light pink scarf, embroidered with shiny silvery threads and the tiniest of pearls forming stunning patterns on it. She held it in front of me, her face beaming with a very pleased smile.

"Absolutely perfect!" she whispered to herself. "Let's wrap it around you."

Again, completely heedless of my nakedness, Edlyn proceeded to wrap the sarong around my waist in an artful fashion. It left just enough of a slit to show off my legs, but not enough to leave my privates exposed. Although it fell slightly above my knees, it perfectly emulated the shorter veil that covered the Thalans' groins and butts.

"How does it feel?" Edlyn asked with a sliver of worry in her eyes.

I took a few steps around the room, crouched, stood up before bending over, then straightening again. "It feels great!"

"So, you're fine with it just around your hips?" Edlyn insisted.

I nodded, heat creeping up my cheeks. She beamed at me again and made a small whooping sound that made me giggle.

"First, we're going to tie up your hair so that I can adorn your body," Edlyn said, while looking at my long locks.

She turned to the box with the shell decorations and opened it. Within, a variety of pearls, shells, and ribbons were neatly separated in little compartments. Edlyn picked up one of the ribbons and bound my hair into a ponytail with it. She then turned to the second box and opened it. I spotted a bunch of small bottles that reminded me of acrylic paint jars. It also had a couple of paintbrushes and a large thing that vaguely resembled a sponge.

"This is going to take a little while. So, if you need to use the hygiene room, now would be a good time," Edlyn warned.

I smiled and shook my head. "I'm good."

"Perfect. Here goes then!" she said with enthusiasm.

She picked up a bottle in the box and squeezed some of the oily substance into her palm. Although subtle, it had a fresh, citrusy scent to it. Edlyn rubbed it between her palms before beginning to apply it over my shoulders, arms, chest, and stomach.

"This will keep the ink from smearing or fading until you are ready to wash it off, even if anything rubs against your skin or if you go in the water," Edlyn explained.

My mother-in-law applied the whole thing with the professionalism and detachment of a therapeutic masseuse. I didn't even flinch or feel awkward when her hands rubbed over my breasts to apply the oil. Although oil didn't feel adequate as there was no oiliness left. My skin fully absorbed it as it would body lotion.

"Now, the magic begins," Edlyn said with a grin after putting down the squeeze bottle.

She picked up a small object that resembled a flashlight and scanned me with it. Once done, she pointed the 'flashlight' at the floor, and it projected a 3D hologram of me. I gasped in surprise. But then a series of colorful tribal patterns appeared on my hologram's skin.

"Pick the pattern you like," Edlyn said.

She began cycling through a different series of patterns.

"They're all beautiful. How do I pick one? And do any of them have a particular meaning?" I asked.

"They don't exactly have a meaning. It's the emotion they convey that matters," Edlyn replied "You see, during courtship, we Thalans create luminous patterns on our skins to seduce our partner. There is no recipe, only our inspiration and things we think will entice the one we covet. As you do not have that ability, we adapted our custom so that you could select something that would convey an emotion you would like to express to your new mate."

I bit my bottom lip, looking at the patterns with new eyes. As she flipped through them, I identified two that really talked to me.

"Is there any way to modify these patterns or to combine them?" I asked hesitantly.

"Absolutely! Which ones?"

I pointed them to her, and she immediately tapped some instructions on the small interface of the "flashlight." The patterns immediately combined, although it now looked a little noisy. But in the next ten minutes, Edlyn eliminated or moved the swirly shapes I indicated until the pattern looked right to me. She then showed me two different color palettes for the pattern: one based on my skin color, the other based on the pink hue of my sarong. Although both looked beautiful, I went with the pink hue.

"This is absolutely gorgeous," Edlyn whispered, her voice filled with emotion. "When I look at it, I feel a sense of hope and freedom."

My throat tightened as I nodded at my mother-in-law. "Yes. That's what Echo and my marriage to him represent to me. Hope for a better future, new beginnings, wild adventures, and a chance at finally belonging."

A strange emotion flitted over Edlyn's face as she looked at me. "He is all that and more. You are home, daughter. Whatever future lies ahead, we are your family."

I quickly blinked away the tears pricking my eyes and gave her a shaky smile.

"Now, let's turn you into a masterpiece," she said with a mischievous glimmer in her eyes. She pointed the 'flashlight' at me, and it projected the pattern onto my skin. "Stand straight and still for a second. It's going to feel a little warm on your skin, but it won't burn."

I complied. Immediately, I felt a rather pleasant heat on my skin, like the gentle caress of the sun at its zenith. Seconds later, the subtle outline of the pattern appeared baked onto my skin.

Edlyn put down the flashlight and took one of the color jars from the octopus box. "This is ink from a vregia, a creature similar to Earth's squids. It possesses the same type of ability we have with our bioluminescent skin cells. When the shadows are applied properly, any source of light will give the impression the pattern is shifting or moving."

She began applying the ink on me with a steady and confident hand. It slightly tickled, but in a pleasant way.

"So… anything special I should know about your son?"

Despite speaking the words nonchalantly, as if merely making conversation, I utterly failed to fool her.

She paused for a second to look at me with a knowing smile, before resuming her work. "There are *a lot* of special things to know about my son. But that, my dear, is for you to discover. That is the most pleasant part of starting a new relationship."

I pursed my lips into an exaggerated pout, which made her laugh.

"Now THAT is one thing you will definitely want to use with my son," Edlyn said with a giggle.

I stiffened, confused. "That? You mean the pouty lips?"

"Mmhmm. You will soon discover that with us females being so few in numbers compared to our males, they tend to be overly protective, and treat us like children. If you ask Echo, he'll probably tell you he's the parent in our relationship."

The way she rolled her eyes made me laugh.

"Well, is he?" I couldn't help but ask.

She chuckled. "I let him *think* he is."

"Why?" I asked, genuinely baffled.

"Because it makes him feel good. It makes him feel like he is needed and that he is performing his duty as a protector," she said with an indulgent smile. "Every Thalan female is completely self-sufficient. We just give them the impression we're dependent on them. They *need* to look after us. It's part of their DNA. Observe our people well over the next few days. You will see it. The challenge is to make your mate feel valued and important without abusing it and without losing yourself either."

CHAPTER 5
ECHO

I smiled at my cousin Raen while he finished securing the crown of shells and pearls on my head. For the past twenty minutes, he'd been showering me with raunchy jokes and warning me that I had better not shame Thalan males as a whole with a poor performance on my wedding night.

Despite my excitement, I couldn't help the worry that had been steadily building since meeting Neera at the spaceport. And Raen knew me far too well for me to fool him indefinitely.

"Now that you're ready, tell me why you're so tense?" Raen said in a severe tone. "I've been spewing one nonsense after the other, and you haven't once told me to go get entangled in a swarm of jellyfish. What's wrong?"

"I'm about to get married. I wouldn't have time to heal your insufferable scaly ass if you did," I grumbled.

He chuckled before quickly sobering. His dark green eyes, a shade slightly paler than his hair, bore into mine as I rose from the stool in his living area.

"All jest aside, what is wrong, Echo?"

I sighed and scratched the scales on my nape, right where my gills ended. "There's nothing wrong, really. I'm just worried my mate is disappointed with me. I mean, she seems to find me agreeable enough to look at but doesn't appear otherwise interested in me."

Raen frowned, an air of concern flitting over his features. "What makes you say that?"

"It's just an impression. She didn't really ask me any questions… You know, the let's-get-to-know-each-other type of questions you usually have with a new partner," I said, my stomach knotting again. "After I finished giving her the tour of the house, there was just this dead and uncomfortable silence. Neera had nothing to say to me and seemed rather relieved when my mother came to prepare her for the wedding. She didn't test any of her siren charms on me or—"

"What of you?" Raen asked, interrupting me. "Did you ask her the let's-get-to-know-each-other type of questions? Did you fill the uncomfortable silence? Did you flirt with her?"

I shifted uneasily on my feet. "I asked her many questions about her journey here, her current health, if she needed rest, food—"

"Those are questions for a tourist visiting us, not your new bride. Did you ask her personal questions? If she likes pets? Her favorite color, food, or pastime?" he asked, interrupting me again.

My scales darkened as I shook my head.

"Have you flirted with her since her arrival on Triton?"

"Yes… Well, I kind of have in a joke while we were flying here. I also told her I found her pleasing to the eye when she was feeling self-conscious about undressing."

I hated my defensive tone as I spoke those words and hated even more the unimpressed look he gave me.

"Okay, fine. Maybe I could have done more, but there just didn't seem to be much chemistry between us. I want this union to work. I just don't know that she wants *me*."

"Then maybe I should take her off your hands if you're going to give up so easily," Raen said with a shrug.

I glared at him, and he gave me the most obnoxiously innocent smile.

"Your mate has been sick. She's probably traumatized by finding herself lightyears away from the only home she's ever known and about to be married to a scaly stranger who failed to come up with a topic of conversation to fill the silence before it became awkward," Raen said matter-of-factly.

"You weren't there. The way she looked at me, my brain just froze."

Raen placed his hands on my shoulders and gave them a squeeze. "Stop overthinking. Forget that she's an off-worlder and forget all that craziness you've been reading about humans. She's a female that you're physically drawn to and who now also happens to be your mate. Just be yourself, and court her like you would any other female. She will never fall in love with who you *think* a human would want you to be, but with who you are. Don't forget, she is a dormant Thalan. Show her why we are the most irresistible males in the known galaxy. Now, let's go get you married… again."

With these words, he slapped the back of my shoulder and led the way out of his dwelling located only a few doors down from mine. My heart filled with affection for my cousin— although I considered him as a brother—as I followed him.

The sun was beginning its slow descent on the horizon. It would take close to two hours before full darkness, and then I would dance for my woman. Raen was right, I needed to make Neera feel properly wooed. I'd been too stiff, too cerebral since our first meeting. I had to show her what a fun, adventurous, and sensual mate I would be to her. I had to make her feel wanted and cared for.

I grinned at the sight of all the tables fully set on the beach, the food cooking on the grill and hot plates, and the pounds of shellfish being placed to chill in the central basin of each table. I thanked my fellow villagers for helping make this possible while heading to the grill. I grabbed and filled a few bowls with cooked dishes, which Raen helped me place on the rotating platform of our table.

Just as I was laying down the plate of oysters, the voices of our females simultaneously rose in a haunting melody. My head jerked up towards my house, and my breath caught in my throat at the sight of my mother, walking hand-in-hand with my mate, bringing her towards us.

I straightened, mesmerized by the stunning pattern drawn on her bare chest and arms, and the beautiful sarong wrapped around her waist. A crown of shells also sat on top of her head, while strings of pink pearls dangled down from it, beautifully contrasting with her dark hair.

"And you said she hadn't used her siren charms?" Raen whispered teasingly next to me, although awe could be heard in his voice.

Neera's Thalan traits were still too dormant for her to fully use her siren's natural talent to lure, mesmerize, and ensnare a male or prey with her charms. And yet, the pattern she had chosen couldn't have been more alluring, and the color palette was clearly a homage to me. I loved seeing my color on her skin. In that instant, I knew that had she possessed bioluminescent skin, she could have enthralled me like none other with only a few shifts of colors and patterns.

I hope she will mutate enough to be able to do it to me someday.

Despite her obvious embarrassment at being the center of attention, the pink on Neera's cheeks also betrayed her excitement. Whatever had happened with my mother had put my mate in a positive mood. I shifted the iridophore cells of my skin that reflect light to say thank you to my mother. Neera—like most creatures, aside from cephalopods—wouldn't be able to see it. I hoped one day she, too, would be able to use this secret method of communication particularly useful underwater.

Mother winked in response as they closed the distance between us, with me meeting them halfway. She stopped only a few steps in front of me then, standing to the side, she reached for my hand and placed the one she held of Neera's into mine. Mother then covered our hands with hers.

The villagers gathered in a circle around us, the hypnotic singing of the females slowly fading.

"Neera Michaels, I give you my only son, Echo Doja, to love and cherish as your bonded mate," Mother said, projecting her voice loudly enough for all to hear her. "Echo Doja, my beloved son, I relinquish you to Neera Michaels. Love, protect, and honor her until your last breath."

Raen approached us with a large conch filled with water that he extended to my mother. She released our hands and took the conch from my cousin.

"May you forever be like water to each other," Mother continued. "A home and a safe haven when the elements unleash their fury all around you. An infinite well to quench the thirst of your bodies and your souls, especially when your hearts feel dry. The current that will always push you forward whatever your endeavors and aspirations, and the still water that will keep you afloat and grant you the peace you crave when you simply need rest."

Mother brought one end of the conch to Neera's lips, who immediately drank a few sips. She then brought the other end to my lips where I also took a few gulps.

"May your union be blessed from this day forward, until death do you part," Mother added while pouring the rest of the water over Neera's and my joined hands. "You may seal your bond."

This time, I turned off my analytical mind and yielded to my emotions. Releasing Neera's hand, I cupped her nape and slipped my other arm around her waist, drawing her to me. My mate's eyes widened for a split second as she understood my mother's word had actually been the equivalent of "You may kiss the bride" from the human wedding. For a split second, I feared she would stiffen or try to pull away from me, but Neera came willingly, lifting her head to receive my kiss.

Before our lips even touched, a bolt of fire exploded in the pit of my stomach at the feel of her naked skin against mine. As soon as my mouth touched hers, a hungry growl rose from my throat. I tightened my embrace around my female, my head tilting to the side. My lips parted, and my mate followed suit, welcoming my invading tongue as I deepened the kiss. I couldn't explain what had taken over me, but the way Neera responded, her hands clinging to my shoulders, and her supple body leaning into me awakened an inferno in my loins.

"Oooh, this should make for a fun wedding night," Mother said mischievously, snapping us out of our daze.

I broke the kiss, my head jerking right so that I could glare at the wretched female.

"Mother!" I exclaimed in outrage while Neera's face turned crimson.

"What? I'm merely stating a fact," she said, eyes wide with false innocence. "But that's for later. For now, your guests need food!"

She patted my cheek as she spoke those words in a singsong voice, then strutted her way to our table. Raen chuckling to my left only had me even more annoyed.

Under the applause of the villagers, I led my mate to the table of honor. I pulled a cushioned stool for her, and she gave me a radiant smile while settling down. I liked that... a lot. I sat next to her, Raen to my right, and Mother to Neera's left. Matriarch Rana sat across from us, next to Raen.

"Neera, please meet my cousin Raen Doja, son of my father's brother," I said to my mate while gesturing at him. "He's beyond insufferable and has made it his life's mission to ruin mine. But he's blood. So, what can you do?"

Neera giggled and smiled at my cousin. "It's a pleasure to meet you, Raen."

"The pleasure is all mine, Neera. But please ignore my cousin. Echo is the one constantly wishing ill on me. And yet, he adores me. He cried like a fingerling when I went to another reef for a few months."

"You mean I wept with relief," I grumbled with false anger, which further seemed to please Neera. She had responded well to me using humor during our flight here. Raen was right. I needed to stop overthinking things and just be myself. "Now stop distracting me so that I can feed my mate."

My mother and the Matriarch chuckled as I rose to my feet to look at the villagers who had all settled at their tables.

"My friends, thank you for this sumptuous feast you have

put together for my union. Eat, drink, and be merry. Today, I have been blessed!"

They all responded with a cheer.

I sat back down, grinning at my mate who was eyeing the bounty of food with undisguised curiosity. While the others at our table started serving themselves, I described each of the dishes to Neera.

"You only have to spin this platform to access the dishes that are out of reach," I said, turning the ring between the stationary center of the table and the edges where we ate. "You should be able to eat pretty much anything here, except these small fishes called perleens or these bigger ones called trotsen."

She wrinkled her nose while eyeballing them. "Considering they are both raw and still covered in scales, that would definitely be a pass for me."

"Hopefully, that's a temporary thing. They are quite tasty," Raen said, grabbing one of the perleens by the tail. He tilted his head back and swallowed the fifteen-centimeter long fish whole.

Neera emitted a squeaky sound then gaped at my cousin, her eyes bulging. "He just swallowed that!"

"It's a small fish," I said hesitantly. "It's like a larger sardine for humans."

"But he didn't chew! Are the bones soft?" she asked, bewildered.

"No, they're quite tough and sharp and far too numerous to be removed," I explained. "Which is why we didn't bother trying to clean and cook any for you. There would be no way to make that fish safe for a human."

"How do they not harm Thalans, then?" Neera insisted, eyeing my cousin with a concerned expression.

Raen chuckled. "I didn't chew it in my mouth because the sharp bones would stab my palate, tongue, and the inside of my cheeks. But I'm chewing it in my throat."

Neera froze, her eyes locked on my cousin's throat as if she was trying to see through it. I shifted uneasily in my seat. Even though we looked human in many aspects, certain parts of our internal anatomy and physiology would undoubtedly be disturbing to my mate.

I cleared my throat, bringing Neera's attention back to me. "Although it doesn't show outwardly, the perleen is indeed getting chewed in Raen's throat. We have a series of very sharp teeth and enzymes that line our throat right below the larynx and most of the length of our esophagus," I explained, feeling a little self-conscious. "They break down bones, scales, and shells. Whatever is left is pretty much mashed into a pulp in our stomach."

My mate stared silently at me for a moment, appearing to be in a bit of a shock, before snapping out of it.

"Wow. Okay. That was… unexpected," she said with a nervous laugh, while casting a strange look at my throat then at my chest.

I would have given anything to know what thoughts were currently crossing her mind. The look on her face made it clear a billion different things were firing off in her head. Wanting to dispel the awkwardness that was rearing its head again with a vengeance, I spun the rotating platform to have the fish stew stop in front of Neera.

"This is seymiak, a seafood soup and one of my favorite cooked dishes," I said with enthusiasm. "I nearly drove my mother insane with how many times I asked for it growing up. Do you want to try?"

"Sure," Neera said, a smile returning to her face.

I happily poured a full ladle with chunky pieces of fish, shellfish, and vegetables. I would have given her more but wanted to leave room for her to taste the other dishes. She leaned forward to smell it, and I caught myself holding my breath while awaiting her reaction. My heart swelled when her eyes widened with a delighted expression.

"Mmhmm, this smells good!" she said with a grin while picking up her spoon.

Under different circumstances, I would have been amused by the similar tension visible on all the faces around the table as my mate was bringing a first spoonful to her mouth. Hospitality was a big deal to us Thalans. That Neera was my new bride made it an even bigger deal for us to make sure she was well-received on her first day among us.

And then she tasted it.

Neera's eyes closed, and the most delectable moan rose from her throat. To my shame, it resonated directly in my groin.

"Oh, my God! That's soooo good! It slightly reminds me of Keralan Fish Stew, although we don't put shellfish in it."

She quickly shoved a couple more large spoonfuls into her mouth while the others around the table chuckled. I just stared at my female with a silly grin and the dumbest sense of accomplishment. I hadn't prepared that dish, but I had fed my female something she greatly enjoyed. That it happened to be one of my favorite dishes only made it even more special.

"Sounds like I will be making seymiak even more often than before," my mother said teasingly.

Neera nodded with a greedy expression that made me laugh.

I poured some of the soup on my own plate, then turned the rotating platform so that my female would have the tray of roasted shellfish in front of her. We spent the next half-hour making her taste a little bit of everything. I made diligent mental notes of what she liked and disliked, and especially of her non-verbal reactions.

My mate had a thing for spicy food, be it raw or cooked— although she appeared to lean towards cooked dishes more. I believed the spices played a big role in it, but also because the food seemed easier for her to chew and swallow. I had never really paid attention to that before, but now, I could see how some of the grilled and raw octopus could be chewy. Even some of the roasted or raw vegetables were too much work for her.

While our teeth resembled those of a human in appearance, their edges were a lot sharper, allowing us to effortlessly bite off the head of a bigger fish like the trotsen in one chomp and swallow it to let our esophageal teeth do the rest of the work. Neera's blunter teeth not only struggled to cut through some of our roots, but also forced her to chew for an unreasonable amount of time to try and get it to a state she could swallow.

More than once, I tried to convince her to just spit out the non-cooperating piece of food she was masticating, but she insisted on soldiering on. As much as it made me guilty, it also increased my admiration for my mate's inner strength and determination.

Still, despite these little bumps, my Neera heartily feasted, finding many dishes, both cooked and raw to her liking. Seeing her eyeing the leftover seymiak with sadness because she was too full to swallow another bite brought another grin to my face. I tossed one last perleen down my throat. Although my mate gave me a subtle sideways glance as I did so, she no longer looked traumatized by it.

With everyone done eating, the males promptly rose to their feet to clear the tables and put in storage all the small amounts of food that had not been consumed. We were pretty good at gauging what was required to avoid waste, especially since we almost exclusively ate fresh. Most of the remaining seafood would be fed to our darters while the leftover cooked dishes would be consumed in the morning.

Under normal circumstances, I would help the others clean the tables, but as I was the groom to an off-worlder bride, my priority had to be looking after her.

"Come, my mate," I said, rising to my feet and extending a hand towards her.

Neera raised an intrigued eyebrow while placing her hand in mine. I loved how warm and delicate it felt. But I loved even more how relaxed and content she looked. I doubted my woman even remembered she was half-naked.

Looking at us walking hand in hand towards the shore, you'd never know we were two perfect strangers freshly joined in a marriage of convenience. I wouldn't say that the chemistry I'd been hoping for had finally shown up, but the absence of awkwardness marked a step in the right direction.

Mother and Matriarch Rana shadowed us while a number of our females entered the water. Raen ran off to the stables to fetch a darter for my mate.

I stopped at the edge of the water and turned to look at Neera. "This is where we part ways. Normally, you and I would perform this dance together underwater, but you will sit on a darter a short distance from the shore and enjoy the show we are—and especially I am—about to put on for you. Prepare to be mesmerized."

I said the last sentence with a playful smugness to hide how nervous I felt. This seduction dance was the real test.

Although my mate wasn't a true Thalan—at least not yet—if I failed to stir her with my siren charm, our chances at a happy union would be slim.

"Mesmerize me, dear husband," Neera replied just as playfully. "I'm all eyes."

I grinned, turned around, and stepped into the water.

CHAPTER 6
NEERA

I couldn't help but smile as I watched Echo walk away. Something had changed in the short time we'd been separated while Edlyn prepared me. The reserved, standoffish man I had first met had given way to a charming, more playful personality during dinner.

And that kiss…

My toes all but curled as I remembered how Echo had kissed me when his mother married us again according to their traditions. A pleasant heat settled in the pit of my stomach as the growling sound he had made replayed in my mind. I could almost again feel his warm, hard body against mine and the gentle way his scales scraped my skin. Goosebumps erupted all over me, and I forced myself to push back those naughty thoughts.

Our wedding night would come soon enough.

For now, not blatantly staring at his stellar behind was the other thing I needed to force myself not to do. He stepped into the water until it reached just above his knees. Despite the darkness quickly falling over us, the crystal-clear water still allowed me to see his calves and feet. Turning around to face me, Echo smiled as he brought his feet together, closing his legs tightly.

My eyes widened, and my lips parted in anticipation as I took an involuntary step forward to get a better view of the spectacle I'd long been waiting for. The scaly patterns on the inner side of his legs suddenly lifted, revealing inner flaps on each leg that ran its entire length. The edge of each flap connected with the one from the opposing leg, stitching seamlessly in the middle, giving the impression Echo had a merman tail. The larger flaps at his hips that had previously crossed in front of his privates into that mini Roman skirt, unfolded, forming flowy fins on each side of his thighs.

He crouched down, lowering himself into the water, then leaned back before pushing off into a backstroke, giving me a full view of him lying on the surface of the water with his merman body. But I didn't get a chance to admire Echo much longer as he turned around, his body undulating as his arms propelled him further ahead and he vanished under the waves.

Countless other males and females also entered the water, all heading straight ahead. A pang of envy shot through me as the urge to join them rode me hard.

At the same time, a series of small spheres shot out into the sky. At first, I believed them to be fireworks, but they didn't explode. Instead, they stopped their ascension fairly low in the sky then flew to a specific position before hovering, their discreet light blossoming into a full glow, lighting up the beach and the water like two dozen mini-moons. Their soft light was perfect to illuminate our surroundings without losing the cozy dimness of nightfall.

Edlyn gently touching my upper arm startled me. I gave

her a questioning look, and she gestured with her chin at Raen approaching the shore, sitting on the back of a darter ray.

"Your ride has arrived," Edlyn said.

I squealed, and clapped my hands with childish excitement, making her laugh. I kicked off my sandals and let her lead me into the water. It was surprisingly warm. Not actually hot, but nowhere near as cold as I would have expected. Just cooler than lukewarm.

The creature awaited me a short distance away. I had water slightly above my knees when I stopped next to it. Good heavens, it was massive, far bigger than I ever imagined. Raen spoke a command in Sikarian, and the creature lowered its right frontal fin—the larger set of two—into the water, turning it into a ramp.

Raen came down the darter and extended a hand to me. "Up you go, young bride."

I took his hand with an excited grin and placed my foot on the creature's fin. My grip immediately tightened around Raen's hand when I realized how slippery the darter's scaly skin was.

"Careful, Neera," Raen cautioned. "If you fall and get hurt, my cousin will feed me to a wobbegong. I'm too young and far too pretty for such a horrendous fate."

I snorted. "Then don't make me laugh, silly man! You'll make me lose my footing!"

"Apologies," he replied without an ounce of sincerity in his voice.

Raen, too, was growing on me. Everything about him screamed pesky little brother and sidekick extraordinaire to my husband. I could see myself becoming friends with him. Holding on tightly to his hand, I gingerly climbed the relatively small incline of the darter's fin, although Raen remained in the water. To my pleasant surprise, the creature helped me out by slowly lifting the tip of its fin while I climbed, leveling the surface to make it easier on me.

Following Raen's instructions, I sat down on the long bump in the middle of the creature's back, folding my knees on each side. It almost felt like I was in the center of my own tiny island. The color palette of the darter reminded me of a coconut octopus. It had a beautiful reddish-brown color, with hints of orange. But instead of the white suction cups lining the edges of the octopus' tentacles, the darter had bright, pale blue specks peppered along the edges of its fins, which gradually faded inward.

I didn't care that my sarong was getting utterly soaked as the crystalline water trickled onto my ride's back to lap at my legs.

"Scoot forward and hang onto the central horn," Raen instructed. "Braga will not swim fast, but better safe than sorry."

I complied, my hands closing around the large horn at the front edge of the bump, where the shoulders ended.

"But how will it know when to stop?" I asked with a sliver of worry.

"Do not worry, Neera. I will swim alongside you and tell him where to stop," Raen said reassuringly. "Now, sit back, and enjoy. Echo choreographed this whole thing specifically for you!"

He didn't have to say it twice. Comfortably seated, I let the creature glide on the surface of the water. Raen and Edlyn —having 'turned' their legs into tails—swam alongside me. Tingling with excitement, I couldn't wipe the goofy grin off my face. Before Kayog, no one had ever gone out of their way to make something super special just for me.

My lips parted in awe as the water suddenly began to bubble in a wide circle about two hundred meters ahead. You'd think a ring of geysers had come to life underwater, although the part of the circle before me was open. In the center, an immense disc of light appeared to be rising from the depths. However, the bubbling ring recalled my attention when the most magnificent creatures emerged from it, resembling some sort of two-legged unicorn seahorses upon which a male or female Thalan was riding, each gender alternating.

The Thalans all began singing an incredibly haunting melody that had wave after wave of shivers coursing through me while my skin erupted in goosebumps. No wonder legend always said sailors could not resist a siren's song. It mesmerized and physically affected me in a way that made my body tingle while also making me languid.

But the luminous circular platform in the middle drew my attention again as it neared the surface. I was so fascinated, I barely heard Raen ordering my darter, Braga, to stop about thirty meters from the platform, and then both he and Edlyn swam away. I couldn't say what the platform was made of. However, it seemed covered in bioluminescent phytoplankton.

A startled gasp escaped me when about a dozen male and female villagers jumped out of the water all around the platform. They performed an aerial flip, during which the flaps of their tails parted again, allowing them to land gracefully on their feet at the edge of the platform. Without pause, they flowed into a dance choreography to the enthralling melody sung by their peers. Among them, Edlyn and Raen were moving with a fluidity and assurance that screamed experience.

For a moment, I wondered where my husband was. The answer came seconds later when a darter ray shot out of the water with a rider on its back. Echo flew around the platform while performing a few acrobatic spins in the air on his mount before diving into the water again. My own squeal of delight as I clapped my hands took me by surprise. But when he emerged a second time, his darter flew above the platform and then flipped itself upside down. My heart skipped a beat when Echo started falling down, as if he had lost his grip on the creature's horn.

The terrified scream that almost rose in my throat faded when he spread his arms wide, legs closed and feet perfectly pointed like an Olympic diver. As he fell towards the platform, Echo folded his body, performing a flawless rotation and landing in a crouched position like superheroes often did in movies.

I lost it, screaming like a crazed fangirl as he proudly stood up, his body gyrating in a sensual fashion to the music. It then registered in my mind that the luminous orbs overhead had significantly dimmed their glow. The twelve dancers accompanying my husband were barely visible anymore, aside from the bioluminescent glow on specific scales of their bodies that almost made it look like luminous patterns were floating in the air all around my mate. While I could see all of Echo, including his features, he also began modifying the color of his scales in a continuous flow that blended seamlessly with the sensuous movements of his dance, as if they were an extension of it.

That, too, stirred a physical response from me. The patterns were not only hypnotic but, added to my husband's movements, they were also turning me on. Oddly enough, the choreography reminded me in part of the Bharatanatyam dance so popular—and actually mandatory—in the South of India. It was the way Echo and the others moved their heads, the undulating gestures of their hands, the positions of the fingers, and some of the poses with their legs and feet. Obviously, it wasn't the same thing, but it still bore some similarities mixed with the sensuality of a male hula dance.

Echo's body was pure perfection. The sinful way in which he moved his hips resonated directly in my core. Before long, I was throbbing, my pulse picking up, and my breathing becoming labored. I'd heard of the Thalans' hypnotic abilities used both to hunt and to seduce a partner, but I never thought they could be this powerful. Although it was an optical illusion, like a kaleidoscope, the bioluminescent patterns on Echo seemed to glow out from his heart, to his limbs and outside of his body into the floating patterns created by the nearly invisible other dancers.

I'd been so mesmerized that I couldn't say if my darter had approached the platform, or if the platform had approached us, either way, Echo was now extending a hand towards me. I rose to my feet on shaky legs, stunned to find him barely a meter in front of me. I took his hand and stepped off the darter's shoulder and onto the platform. It felt soft and spongy under my bare feet. But all such thoughts vanished from my mind as soon as my husband drew me into his arms.

His body felt searing hot against my naked skin. A bolt of desire exploded in the pit of my stomach, intensifying the burning ache between my thighs. A triumphant and predatory grin stretched Echo's lips as he gazed upon my face. For some reason, that messed me up further. His mouth crushing my lips swallowed the needy whimper that rose out of my throat.

The world spun around me, and then water closed over my feverish skin. I should have panicked, but my arms only tightened around my husband's neck, and I wrapped my legs around him as he deepened the kiss. I could feel his hips moving as he flapped his tail, propelling us forward underwater. Each movement made his pelvis rub against my aching core, driving me insane with need.

Moments later, he broke the kiss just as we emerged from the water. I gasped, annoyed with my need to gulp in air when I only wanted to kiss my man some more. His pale eyes had darkened, and the look on his face promised the most exquisite torments as he spun us around in place in the water while I caught my breath. Unable to resist further, I leaned forward and reclaimed his lips.

Echo immediately took over, his tongue diving inside my mouth at the same time our bodies sank underwater. He continued kissing me with a hunger that had liquid fire running through my veins. The only thing that kept me from bursting into flames was the slightly cool water whipping past us as my husband swam at dizzying speed a short distance beneath the surface.

This time, he came back up long before the burning in my lungs would have demanded I come up for air. To my shock, we were already near the shore. Folding his membranes to regain the use of his normal legs, Echo waded out of the water, still carrying and kissing me. I should have been mortified by the chants and applause of the villagers escorting us to the shore, a few of them emitting clicking sounds that vaguely reminded me of those a dolphin or a whale would make.

I didn't care.

Nothing but the feel of my man in my arms, of his possessive hands on me, and of his intoxicating taste on my tongue mattered. I hardly felt the suction of the vacuum of his front porch, even though Echo remained standing there for a few seconds. I didn't see the interior of his house either, our location finally registering in my mind the moment the soft cushion of his bed pressed against my back.

And then it dawned on me that this was the moment things would get real.

The panic I expected did not manifest itself. Panting, I stared at Echo, who was leaning over me with a famished expression. I didn't know why he had suddenly stopped. He was looking at me with an expectant look, as if he wanted me to say something. I just wanted him to continue before my stupid analytical mind kicked in and screwed things over for me. He had me hot and bothered, ready and willing to fulfill my contractual obligations, not out of duty but out of desire. So, what was he waiting for?

I raised my palm to caress his cheek. He closed his eyes and leaned into my touch. The look on his face did the weirdest thing to me, like he ached for my touch, like he wanted to be mine. I lifted my head and kissed his other cheek, my lips trailing down his neck. For an unknown reason, I couldn't resist the sudden urge to run my tongue over the slits of his gills.

Echo hissed, the sound resounding directly into my nether region as he shivered with pleasure. Feeling emboldened, I repeated the gesture, my hand slipping from his cheek to his long, fiery hair. Echo lifted his chin, stretching his neck to give me better access. His soft moan messed with my head. I could not believe I was having such an effect on this beautiful specimen of masculinity.

But he quickly stopped me, pushing me back down onto the bed. He gently caressed my face and my hair—my still fairly damp hair—looking at me as if I were a wonder to behold. He began kissing my face in a slow, gentle fashion: my forehead, my eyes, the tip of my nose, and then my lips.

However, he didn't deepen the kiss, brushing his mouth instead along my cheeks and down the curve of my neck. He lingered there a moment, licking my palpitating artery, gently sucking on my flesh in that sensitive spot that had shivers running down my spine, then down to my collarbone.

Just when I thought he was going to pursue his journey down to my painfully hard nipples, Echo paused again, lifting his head to look at me, his eyes flicking between mine. I understood then without a doubt that he was seeking my permission. I smiled, my fingers tightening their grip in his hair as my stomach fluttered with anticipation.

He didn't return it right away. Eyes locked with mine, his hand roamed from my neck, down my chest and to my left breast. My breath hitched as his palm rubbed over my painfully hard nipple. It didn't linger there, continuing its journey down my stomach and to the delicate knot of my wet sarong. His hand paused there. I swallowed hard, my pulse picking up, making my breathing shallow. I smiled again and licked my lips nervously.

This time, he smiled back. Lying on his side, next to me, his gaze never straying from mine, Echo proceeded to untie the knot with mind-boggling single-handed dexterity. As soon as he finished, he tugged on the fabric, and I lifted my bum to let him pull it from under me. He did so in one swift movement, tossing it somewhere on the floor. Only then did he avert his eyes.

A shiver coursed through me, and my skin erupted in goosebumps again. I couldn't tell if it was due to the cool air of the room on my damp skin or the way Echo's initially tender expression suddenly shifted. As he gazed at the length of my naked body, the same hungry expression he had displayed earlier descended over his features again, making my toes curl.

"My mate," Echo growled, reclaiming my mouth, his hands freely exploring my body with a boldness and a possessiveness that left me reeling.

CHAPTER 7
ECHO

The burning desire had returned with a vengeance. To think I had feared my mate wasn't drawn to me. Her response to my siren charms had exceeded even my wildest expectations. The hunger with which she had looked at me and kissed me after I danced for her had me aching to join with her. Although she had also responded feverishly to my kiss on the beach after Mother bound us, I had wanted to be certain she wasn't yielding to me solely because I'd mesmerized her. And yet, despite allowing the effect of my charm to wane, Neera was still panting for me.

I would see her burn for me.

Surrendering to my hunger, I kissed my mate again, my hands claiming her delicate body. Her scaleless skin was so incredibly soft and warm, so damn sensitive to my touch. And those goosebumps. I wanted to lick them one at a time. But the hardened nubs of her breasts demanded my attention. I loved the sound of Neera's soft moan as I sucked on her nipple, its strange texture tickling my tongue in a delightful way.

I resisted the urge to nip at it. My mate's skin was too soft. Our scales protected us from the sharpness of our teeth. Hers would break too easily. But that didn't stop me from exploring her delicate curves with my hands, lips, and tongue as I made my way down towards my prize.

Neera shivered, her legs tensing and her abdominal muscles contracting as I kissed her sex. The heady scent of her arousal made my length strain against my veil. Finding my mate already wet for me further fueled my desire to claim her. But it would wait. This was our first night. I fully intended to drive my Neera mad with pleasure. I would not allow my female to be disappointed with me as a mate.

With both tongue and fingers, I teased Neera's opening, deliberately avoiding her swollen little nub until she began writhing and begging. Blast! I loved the sound of her needy voice. I no sooner began licking her clitoris than she fell apart. I intensified my ministrations, sucking on her while two of my fingers moved in and out of her, curving up to massage her sweet spot as she surfed the waves of bliss.

Despite our physical differences, it was good that our two species were mostly identical anatomically on the sexual front. Except, Thalan males had a nice little surprise that I was about to spring on my woman.

I settled over Neera. She looked at me through hooded eyes, her face flushed from the pleasure I'd just given her. She parted her legs wider for me while wrapping her arms around my back. As I parted my veil, freeing my shaft at last, I bent my head down to kiss my mate. She passionately returned it, despite the slight tension blossoming through her as she felt my hardness pressing on her. I rubbed myself a few times against her before lowering myself.

Neera tensed a bit more. I considered using my ultrasonic

pulses to make her relax, then thought better of it. Instead, I aligned my *sithai* with her core. My mate stiffened when she felt the bony, vertical ridge on my pelvis press against her. A startled cry escaped her when I made it vibrate, quickly increasing its intensity. I hissed with pleasure when her nails dug into my back, and she arched her head back, an endless flow of moans dripping out of her mouth. There was something powerful about seeing my woman coming apart for me, her hips gyrating under me as my *sithai* vibrated against her clit.

Peppering her face and throat with kisses, I rubbed my pelvis in counterpoint to her movements to increase the friction as Neera began to crest again. She fell apart with a guttural cry that resonated directly in my groin. I clenched my teeth to resist the urge to bury myself deep inside her. Blast! She was soooo beautiful, disheveled, her lips swollen from my kisses, her head rolling from side to side in the throes of ecstasy.

I was doing that to her... to my mate.

While she was still flying high, I slowed down the vibration and carefully began pushing myself inside of her. Even though her body resisted me at first, Neera was still too dazed to tense up as we slowly became one. My *sithai* still massaging her clit kept her from fully coming down. As soon as I was fully sheathed, I bumped up the vibration. My woman cried out, an air of almost painful pleasure settling on her features as she looked at me. I could simply remain like this to make her climax again, but my own restraint had reached its limits.

I began moving in and out of her, slowly at first and then picked up the pace. The feel of her around my shaft was excruciatingly exquisite. A volcano was erupting inside of me, setting my pelvic area ablaze, each stroke sending a pool of lava down my legs and up my spine. Soon, the sound of flesh meeting flesh filled the room accompanied by our sighs of pleasure and voluptuous moans. Neera's hands were all over my body, caressing me and clawing my scales, each touch fanning the inferno consuming me from within. Her mouth on my neck, kissing, sucking, and biting me was driving me insane.

When she first climaxed beneath me, I almost spilled my seed and barely resisted the urge to topple over with her. I cried out and hissed through the burning urge to give in but plowed through. Even as my woman's inner walls convulsed around my length, squeezing me from all sides, I continued to thrust inside her with renewed vigor.

The second time she climaxed around my cock wrecked me. A blinding white light exploded before my eyes as I shouted her name. Liquid bliss shot out of me as I filled my mate with my seed. I felt disjointed, my movements erratic as I kept pumping in and out of her until the last drop was spent.

I collapsed next to her, destroyed. Rolling onto my back, I pulled Neera into my embrace, my arms feeling like jelly while the room spun and wave upon wave of ecstasy continued to course through me. She buried her face in my neck and held on to me possessively.

"My mate," she whispered in a barely audible voice. "My Echo."

Those words filled my heart to bursting. I tightened my hold around her trembling body, her burning skin slick with sweat, and silently swore to never let go of this most precious of treasures.

~

Watching my mate eat breakfast with a healthy appetite filled me with a joy hard to describe. There was something magical about being a provider, caring for someone special, making sure they had everything they needed to thrive, and seeing them blossom under your attentions. My Neera had a very rough start in life, only made harsher by her stalled awakening.

Before her arrival, I had been given a copy of her full medical report. Her difficulties eating and keeping half of her food down had been well-documented. I saw none of it now. Triton was agreeing with her, and so was our food. We'd both had a large helping of leftover seymiak. But I accompanied it with a fresh seaweed and kelp salad as well as a few slices of piaya.

Neera went crazy for the latter.

"Oh, my God! That's amazing!" she exclaimed, after moaning in an exceedingly sensual way as she chewed the fruit. Naturally, that took my mind down a dangerous path. "This has the look and texture of a blood orange but tastes like a mix of mango and pineapple."

"Am I to understand you like these fruits?" I asked, pleased by her reaction.

"Like? I freaking love them! They are among my favorites. I'm really liking this planet of yours," she said, greedily tossing another slice into her mouth.

"This planet of *ours*," I gently corrected. "And I'm glad you are enjoying it. I want you to feel at home here. I want to make you happy."

A soft expression descended over her features. To my shock, Neera smiled then reached across the table to grab my hand. Her fingers looked so small and delicate next to my webbed ones.

"Well, so far, you're doing a wonderful job of it," she said in a voice filled with emotion. "I was both desperate and terrified coming here. I didn't know what kind of welcome I would get here, or if you and I would even get along. I was just praying that we'd like each other enough for this to be tolerable. And, although I can't deny that it was a little awkward at first, something kind of switched when we went through our second wedding. And it has exceeded all of my expectations since."

My hand tightened around hers as my heart swelled with joy. "I felt the same. I was afraid you were disappointed with our pairing and found me unappealing."

"Oh God, not at all!" The disbelieving expression on her face as if I'd said something completely ludicrous moved me even more than her words. "I think you're stunning. I thought *you* weren't that impressed with *me*, and that maybe we didn't have much in common. I tend to overthink and get too much in my head. Once I realize I'm doing it, I try to get out of my own way, but it just makes matters worse."

"And then you're standing there, berating yourself for not saying something to fill the awkward silence. But the more you try, the more your mind goes blank," I said, speechless to realize she'd been going through the same thing I had been.

"And then you start to panic, and feel like you're being an epic failure, which makes your mind go even more blank!" she added, before bursting out laughing.

I joined my laughter to hers, my heart warming further for my female. My thumb gently caressed the back of her hand while we sobered.

"It shames me to admit that I'm relieved you experienced

the same thing I did," I said in a soft voice. "But it also tells me that you and I are aligned. You, too, are exceeding what I had wished for. I have high hopes for our future."

Neera beamed at me. "Well, if you keep pampering me the way you are right now, you will definitely have a very happy bride."

I couldn't help proudly puffing out my chest. "Then I've got this in the bag," I said smugly, while reluctantly letting go of her hand. "Speaking of which, if you are done eating, it is time for me to take you to see Adva."

My mate raised a questioning eyebrow while tossing the last piece of piaya into her mouth.

"She's our healer," I said, while picking up the empty dishes and cleaning the table. "She is waiting to examine you and see how you're handling your first twenty-four hours on Triton."

"Right," Neera said, carrying the remaining dishes to the kitchen—to my great displeasure. "I didn't realize it would start happening so soon."

I took the dishes from her, silently wishing she would have remained seated and just let me take care of her. But then, I had read humans had this thing about sharing the workload equally. An honorable sentiment, but one that wouldn't work for me. Even though we'd just met, I could already tell my mate wouldn't welcome me telling her to let me take care of her—even though she clearly craved being 'pampered' as she said. I would just have to be sneaky about it, doing for her before she had a chance to do for herself. Eventually, she'd grow to see it as the natural order of things.

That thought made me giddy.

"Yes," I replied while washing the dishes—there were too few to justify using my seriously neglected dishwasher. "You must see her daily, at least for this first week. You seem to be adapting well to our atmosphere, but I want to make sure that if anything goes wrong, we'll catch it right away. Your welfare is primordial to me."

That same strange expression—that I absolutely loved—settled on my woman's face again. She stepped closer to me, forcing me to turn from the sink to face her, and wrapped her arms around my waist. She opened and closed her mouth a few times, as if words were failing her. I didn't need the words. Her face was telling me all that I needed.

"I really like you, Echo Doja. I'm glad I was paired with you," she said before hoisting herself to her tiptoes.

I leaned down to kiss my mate, the flame of desire instantly igniting within the second our lips touched. I squelched it. Now wasn't the time to become aroused. I wanted to show Neera the beauty of our world, and I didn't want her thinking I only saw her as a means for sexual gratification. Still, I savored the moment of tenderness with my mate and the lingering taste of piaya on her tongue.

Neera appeared just as disappointed as I felt when I ended the kiss.

"Stop tempting me, you wicked siren," I playfully chastised her.

"Sorry," she said with a chuckle, not sounding the least bit apologetic.

I quickly finished cleaning the dishes then took her hand as I led her to the entrance of the house. This morning, my mate donned an off-white sarong that she prettily wrapped around her waist. While it looked beautiful on her, I couldn't deny missing the pink one she'd worn for our wedding. I had loved seeing my color on her.

Earlier, when I had helped Neera remove the siren pattern

my mother had painted on her last night, my poor mate had been even more distraught than I had been. If she had managed to come up with something this mesmerizing using technology, I could only imagine how powerful her seduction and enticement charms would be should her Thalan genes resume their awakening and she gained bioluminescent skin cells. I would keep wishing for it to happen.

She put on her slippers as we exited the house. Raen had kindly recovered them from the beach, where she'd left them last night before riding Braga into the water, and placed them on our porch. He hadn't asked any questions when we'd met at dawn to harvest some fresh kelp and seaweed. But one look at my face had sufficed for him to know I was happy. He only smiled and gave me a feglite stone—an extremely rare and precious find, meant to guarantee the blissful union of the couple it was bestowed upon. My heart burst with love for my cousin that he should part with such a thing for my sake rather than keep it for the day he, too, would be blessed with a mate.

I gave Neera a sideways glance as she happily smiled and waved to the other villagers out and about. It would probably take a few weeks before we were able to go cast our feglite together, but I couldn't wait. Still, seeing her so relaxed and carefree, apparently oblivious to the nakedness that had so troubled her yesterday further reinforced my hope for a bright future for us.

We entered Adva's clinic to find her and her assistants plowing away in their research lab.

"Ah! There you are," Adva said, using the iridophore cells of her skin to reflect the light in a way that conveyed that message. *"I'll be right there."*

Naturally, Neera couldn't see it, but she understood the message when Adva waved at us through the glass wall of the lab and raised a finger to say one minute. My mate waved back and nodded.

This was something else I really hoped Neera would develop, along with mind-speak. I intended to spend a lot of time with her underwater. Without that ability to communicate, we would have to wear the cumbersome equipment land-bound species used when exploring the depths of our aquatic world.

I led my female to the exit of the lab, the glass walls allowing us to see Adva go through the decontamination process before she joined us in the hallway.

"Decontamination?" Neera asked as soon as Adva came out.

"You should always decontaminate when exiting a research environment where there could be some biohazards."

Neera frowned. "Research? But I thought Echo said you were the healer?"

Adva smiled. "I am. But Thalans do not easily get sick, and Soigo Reef is a very safe area, in large part because we are in a freshwater ecosystem. I can count on one hand the predators that could represent a threat. Most of them are easily incapacitated with our ultrasonic pulses. That means, if I didn't have a side occupation, I would be twiddling my thumbs 90% of the time."

"Ultrasonic pulses?" Neera asked. "I didn't realize you could use them to incapacitate. I thought you guys only used them to detect things nearby or to communicate with each other over long distances."

"We use it for that as well," I said, pleased that my mate had actually read up on us. "But we can also use ultrasounds to stun, put to sleep, or inflict pain to a target. I will show you the pulses' other uses later."

Neera gave me a grateful smile.

"So, when I'm not healing, I'm performing medical research, mainly for improved healing methods against injuries inflicted by some of the most vicious predators found in other regions of Triton," Adva said while leading us towards the medical clinic. "My team and I also work with other planets, especially those that struggle with all kinds of biological crises related to their aquatic fauna."

"Oh wow! That's so nifty! Before I fell ill, I wanted to become a marine biologist!" Neera exclaimed.

"Then you married the right man," Adva said, teasingly.

Neera's head jerked towards me, her eyes wide, her gaze intense with her unspoken question.

"Although I trained as a marine biologist, I'm actually a breeder and trainer," I said carefully. "Today's plan is for me to show you what I do once we're done here."

Neera squealed, shifting happily on her feet while clapping her hands in a way that reminded me of our juveniles. It was unbearably adorable.

"Someone seems excited," Adva said with an indulgent smile. "Let's not delay then and get you examined so you can go wet your feet!"

We entered the medical clinic and Adva led Neera to a medical pod. To my relief, my mate didn't ask me to leave. I'd read humans had a thing about privacy. Instead, she lay down in the pod. Adva closed the dome and typed a few instructions on the interface. As I watched her work, the sudden tension in my spine made me realize I was worried about the potential results. Neera hadn't displayed any sign of discomfort since her arrival here. I'd be devastated if our healer gave a negative prognosis. I was truly growing fond of my mate.

I smiled at Neera through the glass dome. She returned it

before warily eyeing the needles descending to take blood and tissue samples from her. Simultaneously, the device ran a full scan of my female. I gave her a reassuring look before casting a glance at Adva. As was to be expected, our healer wasn't paying attention to me. She focused on her monitor where the data from the scan and sample analysis soon started populating the screen.

Despite my biological training, I was no expert in people, let alone humans. Still, the numbers I could spy on the monitor seemed reassuring. A couple of minutes later, the needles receded and Adva reopened the dome, inviting my mate to sit at the edge.

Neera immediately extended a hand towards me. That she would instinctively seek comfort from me messed me up beyond words. I didn't just take her right hand with my own, I also passed my left arm around her shoulders, drawing her to my side. My mate leaned into me before turning her beautiful gaze expectantly towards Adva.

"Well, the one thing that stands out is your oxygen levels," the healer said in an enthusiastic voice. "They are absolutely stellar, especially compared to your previous levels. Triton is agreeing with you."

Neera nodded while beaming at her. "Yes, definitely. I had forgotten what it felt like not to struggle to breathe. This is amazing."

"You're still a little anemic and have vitamin deficiencies, but the numbers have improved," Adva continued. "We'll be keeping a close eye on that in the upcoming days. You seemed to have a healthy appetite last night. How was it this morning?"

"She was such a bottomless pit, I thought she was going to devour me next," I said.

Neera gasped and elbowed me. "Hardly! I wanted to eat more, but I was too full!"

Adva chuckled with commiseration. "You've had such a hard time eating for so long that your stomach has shrunk. You will likely continue to get full quickly, but don't force it. You'll get back to normal levels soon enough. Just make sure to account for frequent meals. We exert a lot of energy swimming around all day. But while we can feed on the fly underwater if our energy runs low, you can't. Your body has been under a lot of strain. You need to be extra careful while you recover *and* adjust to this new world. Stay well fed and hydrated."

"I will make sure of it," I said very seriously.

My mind was already drawing a list of all the things I could feed my mate and places we could stop for her to rest and eat while we explored Triton.

"Understood," Neera replied.

"Otherwise, I'm not seeing any other changes. Although your mutation is still stalled, I'm not seeing anything that would warrant concerns at this time," Adva said. "But please pay close attention to yourself, both physically and mentally. If you notice any changes, be it skin coloration, rashes, pain or unusual discomforts, sudden mood swings, loss of appetite, or excessive hunger, you name it, come see me. I'd rather we err on the side of caution."

"Agreed," I said forcefully, which made my mate giggle.

"I have a feeling Echo will be dragging me here in total panic every time I sneeze simply because my nose itched," Neera said with fake despair.

"You better believe it," I grumbled.

Despite that, my woman giving my hand a gentle squeeze

as she pressed herself further against me expressed her silent blessing of me watching over her.

After a few more questions and warnings, Adva finally released us once we promised to come back in the morning. On our way out, the healer used her iridophores again to secretly congratulate me on my happiness. I gave her a grateful smile and led my female back to the beach.

CHAPTER 8
NEERA

I followed Echo out with a spring in my step. This arranged marriage business was turning out to be the best thing ever. Beyond the fact that this planet was quite literally saving my life, my husband was hot, super sweet, caring, AND the sex was mind-blowing. I was still reeling from last night. To think I'd feared that moment.

Finding him gone from our bed when I woke up had been a bit of a bummer. Realizing it was so he could have a sumptuous breakfast ready for me had me melting from the inside out. Even now as we walked hand-in-hand on the beach, Echo had the glowing, blissful smile of a happily married newlywed. He was happy to be with *me*, the busted up little nobody that no one else had wanted.

And here I was on an alien beach, lightyears away from Earth, on a planet most people couldn't afford to travel to. Who would have thought I, Neera Michaels, would be carefreely strutting my stuff with my saggy boobs hanging out next to drop-dead-gorgeous arm candy that I got to call mine, and who was equipped with a natural clitoral stimulator that had me singing notes no human vocal cords should ever be able to produce?

Just thinking about it had me hot and bothered. A part of me almost wanted to tell Echo to make a detour home to scratch that itch before going on whatever adventures he had planned for us today. But I squelched that. As much as he'd turned me into a horn-ball, I was eager to get to know more about him and this world. Plus, I had no doubt we'd have another memorable marathon tonight. The wait would only make things more exciting.

We headed to the darter ray stables, although it really looked more like docks with a tall roof, but open on three sides. A bunch of large and heavy containers lined the back wall carved directly into the rock of the mountain surrounding the island. Echo led me to some kind of cabinet and opened the door.

"You can fold your sarong and put it on this shelf," he said, pointing at it.

I complied, suddenly feeling self-conscious again. Since we were going swimming, he made me wear a bikini bottom today. Getting entangled in a sarong didn't sound any more appealing than showing my butt crack and shaved vagina to the entire village. It made zero sense, yet having that sarong instead of just what now amounted to panties, made me feel less naked. Oh well, I'd gotten used to showing my boobs to the whole world, I'd get over this too.

Echo removed a strange-looking object from the cabinet. It looked like the visor of a helmet, but with the upper half made of glass and the bottom half made of a pinkish, spongy-looking material. That same sponge lined the edges of the object. Seeing Echo fiddle with what resembled a pair of straps on one side appeared to confirm my suspicions.

"This is a gill mask," he said, displaying it in front of me. "Off-worlders who come here for special events or for tourism, use similar devices. It allows them to breathe comfortably underwater without requiring a full diving suit. The glass part actually possesses a digital interface that can display text and information, as well as directional arrows. The integrated audio allows them to go on guided tours on their own."

"That's nifty," I said, greedily taking the device from him.

"I had this one especially modified for you," Echo continued, looking pleased with himself. "If you want to ask me questions while we're underwater, simply speak them in your mask. The glass part of the visor will display your words as light signals similar to the ones our iridophore cells produce. You will not see them, but I will. I will respond using my own iridophores, and it will be captured by this camera that will translate it into Universal for you," he added, pointing at the small sphere at the top of the mask.

"But what if you're not looking in my direction when I speak?" I asked.

"Just call my name, and the mask will send an ultrasonic click calling me to draw my attention."

"Wow, I can't believe you went through all this trouble for me!" I said, feeling incredibly touched.

"Of course, I did," he replied, looking at me as if I'd said something silly. "You're my mate. I want you to enjoy your new home to its fullest, even if your mutation doesn't resume. Your happiness is important to me."

My throat tightened, and my eyes pricked. I felt annoyed with myself for getting so easily emotional. But damn, it felt good to have someone so sincerely determined to ensure my welfare.

"You know, if you're trying to make me like you, you sure as hell are doing a good job," I said teasingly to hide what an emotional mess he was turning me into.

"Blast! You're on to me. I'll have to be more subtle in the future," he said with a fake crestfallen expression.

I chuckled and, unable to resist, I closed the distance between us and gave him a hug. He immediately returned it. After a lovely squeeze, he kissed my forehead, the tip of my nose, and then my lips. Echo was a fantastic kisser. Just as I was parting my lips and leaning into my man, two voices, whistling in harmony, startled me.

Echo's head jerked up, and he looked at the two stunning males in the water. They both gave him a shit-eating grin while he glared at them.

"Piss off, you brats, before I spank you both," Echo said in a stern voice.

"Oh! *Now* that you're married, you finally want to do kinky play with us?" the male with pale-blue scales exclaimed, soundly falsely outraged.

I gasped, wondering whether to be shocked or laugh. His companion snorted, and Echo rolled his eyes.

"You both get back to work before I send you to Kaldara," Echo hissed.

Not intimidated in the least by the threat or whatever made that Kaldara place scary, the two males nonetheless raised their palms in a sign of submission, their webbed fingers splayed.

"All right, all right!" the emerald-colored male replied. "Don't get your scales in a tangle! There's no need for such harsh measures."

Both males let themselves sink into the water, just below the surface. Moments later, a pair of darters came towards them, having apparently been called. I gave my man a questioning look.

"Those two insufferable pests are Opire—the green one—and Ouren—the blue one. The fact that they are some of the best pet trainers on Triton is one of the only reasons I tolerate them," Echo said grumpily. Yet the affection in his voice belied his harsh words.

"Well, your cousin Raen also seemed to have a thing about teasing you. Seems to me like you're a magnet for the adorably pesky type of people," I said mockingly.

This time, Echo glared at me with a betrayed expression, which made me burst out laughing. I kissed the corner of his jaw, which appeared to mollify him.

"Raen does tend to join them, and then they gang up on me. That the three of us grew up together certainly doesn't help getting them to show any respect for my authority as their boss," Echo said with a long-suffering sigh that made me chuckle some more.

"Poor sweetie," I said in a commiserating tone.

"Poor me, indeed! At least, now that Opire and Ouren are married, they're too busy building their new home together outside of working hours to make a nuisance of themselves. But they seize every opportunity otherwise."

"Well, I guess I will have to protect you from them!" I offered.

"I would eternally be in your debt, my mate," he said with an excessively relieved expression that had me shaking my head. "But enough with the brats. Let's get you in the water."

Echo helped me put on the mask. The texture of its spongy part felt oddly organic. I almost asked what it was made of then wussed out. I really wanted to enjoy the benefits of this mask and couldn't risk getting creeped out by whatever it turned out to be.

As soon as I placed it over my face—including my ears—the pinkish sponge stuck to my skin, sealing me in hermetically. Thankfully, it didn't do so with the painful tightness of the breathing masks I'd been forced to wear on Earth. Nevertheless, Echo further secured it with a pair of straps around the back of my head.

"Say 'display on' to activate it," Echo said.

The sound of his voice inside the mask startled me, but I complied. It was quite discreet at the top right corner of my screen. Right now, it only indicated the time and temperature. Echo removed another object from the cabinet, this time a bracer which he placed around my wrist.

"This will monitor your vitals, oxygen levels, and buoyancy," Echo explained. "Since you're technically freediving, we need to make sure we don't go too deep and get you into trouble."

It was disturbing to hear his voice inside my mask again when his lips clearly didn't move. That iridophore business was seriously badass.

"Okay, sounds good," I said, eyeballing the interface of the bracer.

"Perfect. Now, let's get you wet."

My head jerked up when I heard his words. Spoken by the artificial voice in my gill mask, it was impossible to say what intonation Echo had intended to convey. His overly innocent look made me highly suspicious this had been a deliberate innuendo. But I would never know.

To my surprise, Echo picked up some sort of backpack from one of the large containers and shouldered it. He then took my hand and led me to the edge of the walkway. We jumped into the water.

Unlike the east side of the island, this section didn't have a slow incline into the water but dropped abruptly into an abyss. There was enough light for me to see clearly the large number of darters lazily swimming below. As we began our descent, a few of them slowly approached, brushing their long, flappy fins against us. Echo extended a hand to caress them as they glided past us. I did the same. The slightly rough texture of their scales tickled my palm.

Considering they were wild, racing creatures, it was odd to see them almost languid as they roamed around. They looked somewhat fearsome with their snake-like heads and the sharp horns on their backs that served as handles. And yet, they were the sweetest, most protective creatures one could find.

Far below, I glimpsed the colorful palette of a coral reef. I didn't need Echo or my bracer to tell me this was much too far for me to dive without a proper suit to regulate pressurization. But a large cave drew my attention. Rune-like symbols glowing with a pale blue light decorated the edge. Darters came in and out of the cave.

By now, as displayed on the interface of my mask, we were just shy of fourteen meters down. I would need to go another ten meters at least to reach the entrance of the cave. While I didn't feel any real discomfort, I didn't want to press my luck so early. As soon as Echo had placed the bracer on my arm, my stats had appeared on the visual display of my visor. Although discreet, I didn't miss how the green light next to the first line was starting to turn yellow. I went down a couple more meters before stopping.

"Too much?" Echo asked.

"The bracer seems to say it wouldn't be wise for me to go much further down," I said, disappointed.

"No worries. If you can't go to the cave, the cave will come to you."

It seriously fucked with my head to see him smiling encouragingly while the neutral voice translated his silent words. It was almost the same uncanny feeling one got when watching a ventriloquist. But at least, their tone conveyed the emotion the doll acted out. This just broke my brain.

Echo focused on the cave then a series of clicking sounds emanated from him. Although I understood them to be ultra-sonic sounds, I had expected him to make them with his mouth. But once more, his lips remained sealed. How did he make those sounds? And how come I could hear them? I'd always assumed echolocation sounds were at a higher frequency than the human ear could perceive, like dog whistles.

But all those questions flew out of my head seconds later when two dozen baby darters came out of the caves like translucent bats out of hell. Echo grinned while removing the backpack from his shoulders. He opened it, shoved his hand inside, grabbed a handful of something that he tossed into the water surrounding him. I assumed they were some sort of treats for the younglings, but I was too mesmerized by the babies to really pay attention.

Just like Earth's baby manta rays, the little darters looked like little frogs trapped inside translucent raviolis. However, they appeared to have captured a plasma ball inside their bodies as slow lightning-shaped tendrils coursed through the translucent fins that gave them that ravioli appearance.

They raced after the treats Echo had released. At first, I'd assumed the current was carrying them away, but the pattern in which the treats moved was too scattered. Sadly, the babies swallowed them all too quickly before I could properly inspect them.

Echo extended the backpack towards me before lifting the flap. On instinct, I stuck my hand inside to grab a fistful of treats. But even as I began drawing my hand out, a billion wiggling sensations against my palm and fingers had me yanking my hand out with a yelp. To my horror, the 'treats' I'd thus released immediately tried to scatter. Their plump, ringed, grayish bodies reminded me of a short caterpillar. They deployed tiny fins—akin to those of a flying fish—and flapped them in a frenzy in their vain attempt at a getaway.

"Oh, my God! Oh, my God!" I exclaimed, rubbing my palm frantically on my thigh to erase the crawling sensation I could still feel on my hand.

Echo burst out laughing upon seeing my reaction. I wanted to punch him in the throat but was still too busy freaking out. He finished distributing the 'flying maggots' before shouldering the backpack again.

A number of adult darters were circling around us, clearly keeping watch so none of the little ones would stray too far, but didn't otherwise interfere. I was pleasantly surprised to see the babies playing nice, none bullying another in order to get more treats.

By the time they were done eating, they closed in on us, rubbing more closely against us than their parents had done earlier. About the size of a large dining plate, they wrapped their flappy fins around us in the equivalent of a hug, and rubbed their snake heads on us, before letting go. One settled on my back and poked my nape a couple of times in what felt akin to a kiss. The lightning under their skin made my own tingle and even tickle depending on where the youngling was hugging me.

I couldn't tell how long it had lasted, but it felt like I'd just been touched by the physical incarnation of infinite love, innocence, and blind trust. I'd been fascinated by darter rays the very first time I read about them. But now, I was truly in love with those fascinating creatures.

As the parents started herding the little ones back inside the cave, Echo led me to the surface, forcing me to follow a low-angled, ascending diagonal line rather than go vertically. I didn't think it was all that necessary, but this qualified as a situation where it was better to err on the side of caution. That took us farther away from the stables or the beach. To my surprise, Braga had followed us. As soon as we reached the surface, he stopped beneath us before rising, turning into a platform we could sit on atop the water.

Echo scooted closer to me, and we kneeled face to face, our legs on each side of the bump on Braga's back. He leaned forward and detached the straps securing the mask to my face. I eyed him questioningly as soon as the mask came off.

"You can't wear this for more than a couple of minutes outside water," Echo explained. "The gills from your mask are similar to those of a fish. They can only draw oxygen from water. So, when you're no longer submerged, you're using up the oxygen trapped inside the mask and replacing it with carbon dioxide. You would eventually pass out."

"That's no good," I said, scrunching my face.

"I thought you'd feel that way," he said with a chuckle.

I eyed his backpack and scrunched my face further. "What the heck were those gross things you made me touch?"

Echo laughed. "They're not gross. They're called ubrils."

"They looked like winged caterpillars," I said, still frowning.

"Actually, they're more like finned maggots that are very high in nutrients." He chuckled when I dry heaved. "Aww come on, it's not that bad. I find shrimp more repulsive in appearance, and far more demanding to eat. Ubrils are a little chewy and sweet."

"How the heck would you know what they taste like?" I asked, horrified by the answer I already knew was coming.

He shamelessly grinned. "Because I ate some, of course. They possess a fairly toxic venom sack that isn't harmful to us. They are great for our babies—including darters—as the toxin kills bacteria that can cause a variety of infections, especially before our scales are fully formed. It is a treat for younglings. Adults rarely eat them, except to help fight certain infections."

"Well, that's still going to be a hard pass for me," I mumbled, which only made him laugh again. "Aside from those gross critters, that was awesome. Those babies are freaking adorable. I hope to be able to go see them directly inside their cave one day."

Echo grinned proudly. "I'm sure you will, sooner than later. But for now, Braga will take us to the other side of the island so that I can introduce you to our peridorns—the other creatures I train."

I squirmed where I sat. "Err.. Actually, could we drop by the house first before we go there?"

Echo instantly became alarmed. "What's wrong? Are you hungry? Tired? Are you feeling unwell?"

"No, no! Nothing like that," I said, raising my palms in a reassuring gesture. "It's just… I need to make a pit stop."

He blinked, clearly clueless as to what I meant. I cringed inwardly.

"I need to use the hygiene room," I said, my cheeks heating.

He appeared baffled at first, then understanding dawned on him. "Right. The ditches are too deep for you. Let's go home, then."

"The ditches?" I asked, confused.

"When in the water, there are the places where we go to relieve ourselves of solid wastes while helping the ecosystem thrive," Echo explained. "Coral reefs are usually a safe bet, but there are other places I will eventually show you when your body can handle greater depths."

This time, my cheeks felt on the verge of bursting into flames as I shook my head. "I only need to pee. But you guys actually poop in the water?!"

He looked at me as if he was questioning my IQ. "Obviously, yes. Why swim all the way back home when we can do it nearby while providing essential nutrients to the local flora and fauna? Don't forget that we're sometimes days away from any island or floating city."

"Right, but..." My voice trailed off as I failed to find any proper argument.

"But nothing, silly woman. It's natural. However, I'm confused as to why you didn't relieve your bladder if you simply need to urinate," he said, giving me a strange look. "Surely humans do it when they go swimming in a lake, river, or at the beach?"

You better believe it, and especially in public pools.

And I thought of doing it about a billion times, too, the minute my stupid bladder started acting up. But how was I supposed to tell him that I had not dared for fear his overly sensitive Thalan abilities would detect it the minute I did? For all I knew, peeing in the water near him would be like that silent fart you released, hoping no one would notice, but that ended up stinking worse than a thousand corpses under a burning sun.

"Yes, but we usually swim away from anyone nearby to do our thing discreetly," I mumbled, dying with embarrassment. "It would have been rather disrespectful for me to pee right next to you and have you swimming in it."

He chuckled and slowly nodded. "We also consider that rude. As you said, you are expected to swim a little distance away to 'do your thing' before returning to the group. But I guess I did follow you pretty closely to make sure you were fine."

I nodded. Escape definitely wouldn't have been a possibility.

"I bet you feared I'd detect it, if you did," he added teasingly.

The crimson shade of my face gave me away, making him laugh a bit more.

"Would you? Would you have noticed if I did?" I asked sheepishly.

"If you did it near me, yes, I absolutely would have known," he added with a mocking expression.

Thank God I'd followed my gut and held it in!

"For what it's worth, I wouldn't have minded," he added gently.

I made a face at him. "You wouldn't have minded swimming in my urine?"

"I wouldn't have minded being exposed to a tiny amount of it, mostly diluted in the water and carried away by the current," he said. "I mean, we spent the past fifteen minutes being hugged by a bunch of darter ray fledglings that happily showered us with their liquid and solid wastes."

My eyes nearly popped out of my head as my jaw dropped. Echo burst out laughing at my flabbergasted expression.

"You're just saying that to freak me out," I challenged.

He shook his head. "No, I assure you I'm not. Adult darters will move away to do their business, but babies are babies and let go whenever, wherever, as soon as the need hits them. These little ones simply don't happen to wear diapers."

"But... but I didn't see anything!"

"Because at their size, it is very small. Like many fish, the young darters get rid of waste through their skin and gills. Although some do it through pores near the rear of their bodies. That is the case of adult darters. But..."

His voice faded when he saw my horrified expression. My brain had barely registered his last words, remaining stuck on his comments about eliminating waste through their skin and gills. Echo looked down at himself, wondering for a second what I was staring at before his face lit up with understanding. He barked a belly laugh that would have also cracked me up under different circumstances.

"No, Neera, I'm not a fish. I do not excrete feces through my gills. We are very much like humans on that front. So, you were not giving me a cunnilingus last night when you licked my gills."

"Oh God!" I whispered, burying my face in my hands, mortified. Of course, the fiend had guessed the source of my horror.

"You are beyond adorable. But I've teased you enough for now. Go on in the water and do your business. I promise neither Braga nor I will take offense."

I wanted so badly to throw something at him and that obnoxious grin of his. However, pride and embarrassment both needed to take a backseat. Neither warranted me needlessly torturing myself. I swam a short distance away before diving down. While my bladder welcomed the relief, I still hated that my man knew that I was taking a piss in the water. Oh well, I'd gotten over bare boobs and strutting in a bikini bottom. I'd get over this, too.

CHAPTER 9
ECHO

My mate was unbearably adorable. I had wondered what it would be like to be mated to an off-worlder. As our descendants, humans shared a lot of similarities with us that had made certain things easier. But as landbound folks, they greatly differed on other fronts. Helping Neera adapt to this new world was helping me rediscover the beauties not only of my planet, but also of my own species.

Before her, I never questioned or really thought about our unique traits and abilities that helped us thrive in our world and that other species lacked. I struggled to understand how Neera and her people in general managed with so many physical restrictions, on land but especially in the water.

Unless they wore a protective mask, they couldn't open their eyes underwater without risking severe injury over time. And even then, they'd be considered half-blind by our standards. They had no real way of communicating naturally. They would quickly suffocate or drown without an artificial breathing method. They couldn't handle more than a short depth without suffering from water pressure. They possessed no instinctive methods of orienting themselves, had very few defensive or offensive traits, and suffered from a ridiculously limited endurance on top of slow swimming speed.

All this made me worry to no end for Neera's welfare. I didn't want to smother her with my overprotectiveness, but too many things could easily go wrong for her. I desperately needed my woman to resume her mutation so that she would be safer among us. I couldn't bear the thought of any harm coming to her. Worse still, I wanted the dreadful image of my mate drowning permanently cast out of my mind. Until Neera got her own set of gills, I wouldn't be able to breathe easy— no pun intended.

But right now, watching her make the acquaintance of our peridorns had me melting from the inside out. I'd worried that she wouldn't be a pet lover. Granted, both the darters and peridorns were mild-tempered creatures and generally pleasing to the eye. Still, my woman was a natural. She exuded a loving aura which the creatures perceived and which drew them to her. Even now, Yoni was gently rubbing the side of her scaly snout against Neera's cheek in an affectionate gesture.

She was magnificent with her midnight blue and magenta scales, her somewhat lizard-like head with a single horn on the forehead, and majestic three-meter-long tail. Neera called her a seahorse mount. I never quite understood why humans called a hippocampus a seahorse. The resemblance with an actual horse or the mythological creature it was named after was quite slim. And it was even slimmer in our case considering their seahorses didn't have legs or arms, whereas peridorns possessed two front legs with webbed paws.

"While they can swim at the surface, like they did for the dance at our wedding, peridorns almost exclusively dwell underwater. They especially thrive in great depths," I explained.

"So, what do they do?" Neera asked while caressing the flowy membranes that shaped the mane of the creature. "Are they like the standard transportation in your underwater cities?"

I chuckled and shook my head. "No. We normally just swim around. However, we do ride them usually to travel great distances underwater, especially in saltwater as they prefer more saline environments, unlike darters. Peridorns are also excellent rescue pets. Their front paws allow them to open doors, dig where is needed, grab onto something or someone to pull them out of a difficult spot, and their long tails can wrap around bigger objects to lift that obstacle."

"Oh wow!" Neera exclaimed, looking at Yoni with new eyes. "They're like super underwater search and rescue dogs."

I nodded. "They are extremely intelligent. Not to the point of having a conversation, but they can make critical decisions on their own when it comes to rescuing an individual or another creature. They also have echolocation and will send a distress signal when they find something or someone."

"That's really impressive. But how often do you need their assistance?" she asked.

"On Triton, very rarely. Here, we mostly use them in competitive settings for scavenger hunts. We sell them to a number of other planets, including our homeworld, Sikaria."

Neera frowned. "I thought Sikaria had a different atmospheric pressure. Wouldn't that negatively impact the peridorns?"

I smiled at my mate. "Excellent question. But no, peridorns are highly flexible creatures. Their physiology adapts to their new environment. Among other things, they have a second pair of lungs that they barely use here on Triton, except when they go to extreme depths. On Sikaria, they simply always use both pairs."

My mate grilled me with a few more questions. I loved her genuine curiosity and enthusiasm about my work. But it was seeing her playing with one of the younglings that messed me up. With their long tails and front legs, they bore an uncanny resemblance—shape wise—to our own finger-lings, who spent most of their young years with their legs stitched in a tail. The way she held the little male cradled in her arms, slowly rocking him while making cute but nonsen-sical sounds at it, awakened a brutal longing within me. What I wouldn't give to be a father and for this to be our offspring she was holding.

According to Dr. Atani—the Sikarian physician who had seen Neera back on Earth—awakened humans were more fertile than pure born Thalans. I'd been beside myself with excitement upon hearing that news. But she'd also cautioned me that this was true of the awakened humans that had fully mutated. With Neera's transformation being stalled, would the same be true?

When we returned home, my mate insisted we go rinse at the waterfall, and that we should do so every day from now on. She refused to walk around with 'poopy-pee' water clinging to her skin. Silly female... I happily indulged her, especially since she let me rub her down while she rinsed. But I didn't doubt she'd eventually get over it.

Although we only took a few minutes, by the time we strolled back to the house, Neera suddenly looked quite tired.

"Are you all right?" I asked with a sliver of concern.

"Yeah. I just got super tired out of the blue. I think I need a nap," she said sheepishly.

"I should be the one apologizing. I made you overexert yourself," I said, silently berating myself. "You've been sick, and I made you frolic all day in the water, knowing that swimming works pretty much every muscle in your body. I'm sorry. I will do better."

"Don't be silly," Neera said, frowning at me as we stepped onto the porch, standing there a few seconds to let the vacuum perform its magic. "You have taken every precaution to keep me safe, including that bracer. And I'm a grown adult. If there was a problem, I should be the first one to speak up."

"But it's my duty—"

Neera pressed two fingers to my lips to silence me. "Enough. You're not to blame. Frankly, there is nothing to recriminate about. Yes, I'm feeling exhausted, but it's the good type of tired. The one you get after an excellent work out, especially if you've been slacking for a while. That means I'm going to sleep like a baby during that nap."

"Fine, but I'm still carrying you to bed," I mumbled, picking her up.

I expected Neera to protest. To my pleasant surprise, she snuggled against me, burying her face in my neck. Blast! I loved when she did that. There was something so affectionate and trusting about that gesture that always moved me deeply.

It was only when I laid her down on the bed that Neera finally protested.

"My hair is still quite wet. It's going to mess up the mattress and pillow," she mumbled, fighting not to doze off.

"Don't worry about it. They are made specifically to handle that. Rest, my mate," I said, climbing onto the bed next to her.

Neera once more curled up against me, placing her head on my chest. I didn't need to sleep, but watching over my woman while she slept felt right. Gently caressing her hair, I mentally made plans for the next few days for us.

~

The next three days flew by in the most wondrous dream. Raen, Ouren, and Opire picked up a lot of my slack, allowing me to devote most of my time to Neera, teaching her the basics of training darters. They were a lot easier to ride and control, on top of having the major advantage of dwelling in shallower waters. It spared Neera from having to wear the gill mask too often.

Today, she was helping me train Piri, a young darter female that was promising to become a fierce and speedy racer.

"During a competition or a hunt, your rivals—or potentially your prey—may try to cut you off or charge you. You must not panic. And above all, you must keep your darter from panicking," I explained. "Rubbing your mount's shoulders around the handle horn will help appease them. But you don't have to worry about that for now, because *you* get to harass *me*."

"Is that so?" Neera asked, a mischievous glimmer in her eyes.

"Mmhmm. Braga is a seasoned hunter. Piri has already gotten some training but still has a long way to go," I said. "I will try to flee. Cut us off in the most ruthless ways you can."

"Isn't it going to distress her?" Neera asked, looking worried.

My face softened. Her instinctive concern for the creatures

pleased me tremendously. Off-worlders were often callous when it came to their entertainment, not worrying about anything other than their personal enjoyment.

"No. I will help her manage her emotions, and Braga will not push her too far, no matter how wild *you* may get," I said reassuringly.

"Good, because you *know* I'm going all out on you," she said with a fiendish grin.

"Bring it on, my dear. Bring it on!"

With a gentle pressure from my knees on each side of her dorsal mound—which served as a seat for the rider—I prompted Piri to start moving just at the surface. A sustained squeeze told her to keep going faster until I relented.

Soon, we were surfing at a nice speed, and Neera came at us with a vengeance. She had Braga zip past us before making a sharp turn right in front of us. Invariably, Piri would abruptly veer to the opposite side or dive. While the dives weren't so bad, the veers systematically got me thrown off her back. Sure, I could have held on to her horn not to fall, but that would have hurt her.

Naturally, Neera took great pleasure at seeing me take one dive after another. She even started counting out loud the number of times I fell off as soon as I resurfaced. When Piri finally began reining in her instinctive flight impulse, they changed their tactics. They startled her by diving and jumping out of the water either right in front of us, or close enough on Piri's flank. Despite the grumpy faces I made at Neera, I was having a blast, and so was she. On top of it all, Piri was getting awesome training.

I'd just once again crawled out of the water onto Piri's back for another round when Braga emitted a loud hissing growl—the darter's way of sounding the alarm. My blood turned to ice as my head jerked in his direction, and I saw him a good fifty meters away, diving without Neera on his back.

"No!" I whispered, ordering Piri to dive as well.

The darter raced underwater towards their location. To my horror, Neera appeared to be both trying to swim back to the surface and fighting against an invisible enemy. The way her body shook, she was either in severe pain or victim to violent spasms.

And she was drowning…

Braga attempted in vain to glide under her and lift her to the surface, but the way she fought and contorted her body kept making her fall off his back. I jumped off Piri as she swam past Neera, who had sunk at least ten meters down. I rushed to her side, earning myself a few solid punches and kicks from my panicked mate. When I finally managed to wrap my arms around her, she nearly bashed my face in with the back of her head.

I emitted three ultrasonic pulses in quick succession, channeling them down my chest and against her spine. Neera immediately went limp. While racing to the surface, I sent out a series of distressed clicks towards the village so that anyone in the water by the beach could go warn Adva of our imminent arrival.

Even as I breached the surface, Braga slipped under us, providing me with the much-needed platform to tend to my mate. He didn't need me to say anything to know he was to head back to the shore. As he glided home, I turned my mate onto her stomach and pressed my palms to her back in an upward movement to purge the water out of her lungs. Despite the fear choking me, having previously performed such a rescue on off-worlders over the years allowed me to function rationally instead of completely losing it.

The great amount of water that poured out of my mate frightened me. But then Neera suddenly started coughing while the last of the water dripped out of her mouth. I could have wept with relief. However, something was terribly wrong with my mate. Her skin should have been cool, but it was literally burning. Between two bouts of coughing, she moaned in pain and seemed to be on the verge of convulsing.

Thankfully, the shore was getting closer. I gathered her in my arms and jumped into the water as soon as we arrived. Mother and Raen were standing by the beach along with a few other worried villagers. I raced towards the clinic. Adva was already waiting in front for us.

I ignored the hover stretcher next to her and just ran inside the building, making a beeline for the clinic. I laid my woman down inside the medical pod we'd been using since her arrival to perform diagnostics on her.

"I don't know what happened," I said in a panicked voice as I stepped aside to let Adva examine Neera. "One minute she was fine, the next she had fallen off Braga and was drowning. She's burning up and appears to be in pain."

Adva pressed a hypospray to Neera's neck, and my female immediately relaxed. Although she stopped moaning in pain, and her face no longer showed any signs of distress, her body continued to be shaken by light spasms.

Watching the healer work diligently—and far too quietly —on my mate had me nearly climbing the walls. I understood that she couldn't tell me anything until she had a better idea of what was happening, but I needed some kind of reassurance. A soft hand on my shoulder startled me. I noticed then that

Mother had followed us inside the room. Raen had remained outside.

I pulled my mother into a desperate embrace. She gently caressed my hair while humming in the way that always appeased me growing up. I eventually released her, feeling both sheepish and grateful. She merely smiled and caressed my cheek.

"Well, even though this looks scary, there's no reason for alarm," Adva said with a world of relief in her voice.

"What do you mean? She's burning up and in pain!" I challenged, not yet willing to give in to hope.

The healer nodded. "Yes, she's burning up and in pain because her mutation has resumed."

"Why in pain?" Mother asked. "Is something wrong with her mutation?"

"No, not at all. The pain is normal. After all, her DNA is getting rewritten, and her body is transforming at an extremely high speed. It is bound to be incredibly painful," Adva said in a gentle tone. "All of her readings match the standard ones Dr. Atani sent me from the other humans awakening."

"Fine, but how do we alleviate her pain?" I asked, hating to see my female like this.

"You will need to keep her nearly unconscious with your ultrasonic pulses and strum for her whenever she shows any signs of pain," Adva replied.

"Strumming works on humans?" I asked, my heart soaring.

Adva smiled. "Yes, that's the method they use on Earth. Each phase of the mutation normally lasts about forty-eight hours, sometimes a little shorter or longer. In Neera's case, it's impossible to say for sure."

"She will be a full Thalan in two days?" Mother exclaimed in an excited voice.

"No. There are multiple phases. Technically, this should be Neera's first phase, but she already sustained some mutations, but not all of the ones usually included in it. So it's hard to say if this will simply complete her first phase, or overlap with the second," Adva explained.

"What does the first phase entail?" I asked.

"The awakening humans quickly acquire a series of Thalan traits, mostly the 'external' ones like scales, gills, and tail," Adva said. "But with Neera, her lungs were the first to mutate on Earth, which usually occurs at the end of the first phase. So, it's really hard to say what will happen with her now. Then things should slow down for a couple of weeks before the second phase begins; that will unlock echolocation, mind-speak, and her bioluminescence. The third will finish modifying her internal organs and make her a full Thalan."

I felt dizzy; relief, excitement, and lingering worry flooding through me. "Very well. I shall keep her unconscious and strum. Anything else I can do to help her?"

"Yes," Adva said while retrieving a box from one of the cooling units. She extended it to me. "This box contains hypodermic syringes. They contain a cocktail of proteins and nutrients that Neera's body will need for a smooth transition."

"How often should I inject her?" I asked, holding the box as if it were the universe's greatest treasure.

"This bracer will let you know," the healer replied, showing it to me before placing it on Neera's wrist. "It will beep whenever an injection is needed. It will also allow me to monitor her vitals in real-time. So, if anything goes wrong, I will be immediately alerted."

Those last words sent another massive wave of relief over me. "Thank you," I said with sincere gratitude.

She smiled in an almost motherly fashion. "Note that Neera will doze in and out of consciousness over the duration of her mutation. Every time she wakes, make her drink water. It is important to keep her well hydrated. As soon as she displays the first sign of pain or discomfort, put her back to sleep."

"Will do," I said, swallowing hard as I looked tenderly at my mate.

It was crazy how deeply that female had gotten under my skin. I couldn't bear the thought of losing her.

After a few more instructions, Adva allowed me to take Neera home. Once again, I refused the hover stretcher. I handed the box of hyposprays to my mother and carried my woman in my arms, where she belonged. Somehow, feeling her body against me—overheated though it was—had some sort of soothing effect on me. I hated all the unknowns surrounding her current state, and yet hope blossomed inside of me. She was becoming more like us. Triton was claiming her for me.

"Take your mate to bed and make her comfortable," Mother said in a gentle yet surprisingly firm voice as soon as we entered my house. "Raen and I will take care of everything else."

I didn't argue and headed straight to our bedroom where I carefully laid Neera down onto the mattress. After setting her down comfortably, I climbed onto the bed behind her, pulling her body against mine. Aligning my chest with her back, I immediately began to strum. Through my chest, the vibration also sounded like a melodic buzzing that I could modulate to a certain extent. The vibrations seeped through my mate's body, down her spine and to her nerve endings, numbing them and silencing any pain and discomfort she might feel. Neera's body relaxed against mine, the spasms fading, and her breathing settling to a calm and regular pace.

After a discreet knock, Mother and Raen entered the room. She placed the hyposprays on the nightstand while my cousin brought a pitcher of water with a glass and a straw. He squeezed my shoulder and gave me an encouraging smile before exiting the room.

Mother sat down on the bed next to Neera. My throat tightened as she stared at my mate with the same maternal tenderness she used to look at me with the few times I got sick growing up. She gently caressed Neera's cheek with her knuckles before leaning forward to caress my forearm.

"I can sense your fear, my son," Mother said in a soothing voice. "Cast it aside. All is well. She was made for you. I can feel it in my bones. Neera is becoming what she was meant to be. And that will make her the perfect mate for you. It was fate that brought her halfway across the galaxy to us... to you. Now, she needs you more than ever to help her through this difficult transition. Look after her, I will look after you, and Raen will look after your pets. Neera is the only thing that matters right now. Strum for your mate, surround her with your love, your hopes, and the joy you have filled her life with over the past week. Think of how beautiful her scales will be, and the look on her face when you take her to our sunken city."

"She's going to love it," I said, my heart filling with gratitude for my mother.

"Yes, she will... like everything else you've shown her so far. You are a good mate, Echo. Your birth was the first great blessing in my life. Every day since, you've been my greatest pride and joy. And now, you've blessed me with a beautiful daughter. Do not fret, my son. All will be well."

"I love you, Mother," I said, my throat almost too constricted to speak.

"I love you, too, my darling."

She leaned over to kiss my forehead, then kissed Neera's forehead before quietly leaving the room.

CHAPTER 10
ECHO

The next forty-eight hours proved the most excruciating of my entire life. Witnessing my mate's transformation in real time was both exhilarating and unnerving. Despite being born a Thalan and undergoing the different stages of growth of our species, Neera's mutation was still traumatic to me.

With her burning fever that came and went on a whim, Neera's skin had felt clammy to the touch. But it wasn't long before it started taking on a shiny color that I realized its very texture was changing. Where human skin was thin and soft, ours was thicker and slightly rubbery. Neera had compared mine to that of a dolphin. And hers was transitioning to ours. The shininess of her skin, making it almost look like gold, corresponded to the pre-scale state. Had I not gone through it myself growing up and seen it regularly on our young, I'd be freaking out.

Right now though, her skin looked raw and painful. Having Adva confirm it was indeed the case did nothing to make me feel better. At least, my strumming kept the pain at bay. It wasn't the scaleless state that made the skin overly tender but the fact that it was mutating to allow her to thrive at greater depths and in much colder waters. I would miss her delicate human skin, but the benefits of this new one outweighed my selfish sense of loss.

The few times Neera woke up, I barely had time to make her drink a few sips of water before I had to use my sonic pulses to put her under.

The round edges of her ears looked inflamed as they began to stretch into our long, fan-shaped ears. Her fingers and toes, too, appeared swollen as a fine webbing began forming between them.

By the end of the first twenty-four hours, Mother had threatened to have Raen, Ouren, and Opire drag me out of the room and shackle me to the dining table if I didn't pause for a moment to eat. I only caved when she agreed to let me eat, sitting near Neera in the bedroom. The fiendish female had prepared seymiak, making it impossible for me to resist.

On the second day, in the early afternoon, Neera's scales began forming. They were still dull and somewhat translucent. But I could already tell they would be a stunning burnished gold or light bronze color. To my dismay, as the sun began setting, my mate was clearly nowhere near being done with this phase of her mutation. When her bracer beeped, I picked up another hypospray and brushed aside her long hair —whose texture had also changed to match our more impermeable locks. But I froze upon seeing the delicate slits of her gills beginning to form on her neck.

"Oh, my mate," I said, my heart soaring.

The image of her drowning while Braga and I tried to

assist her had replayed in a loop in my head. I never wanted Neera that vulnerable again. These would finally give me the peace of mind—or at least some of it—I desperately needed where she was concerned. I carefully ran a finger over them before leaning down and gently kissing them. I then pressed the nutrient hypospray to her nape and injected her.

By the end of the third day, I was losing my battle against sleep. I was kicking myself for not napping all the times my mother had forced me to take a break to eat, drink, hydrate at the waterfall, and use the hygiene room. But I'd feared falling into a deep sleep instead of caring for Neera. With her scales now fully formed, including her veil and the tail membranes on the inner sides of her legs, my woman could awaken any minute now. During my last forced break, Mother seized the opportunity to wash Neera. I managed to stay alert through that, eating helping me in achieving that nearly impossible feat. However, the minute I laid down behind my mate, ready to strum again at the first sign of distress on her part, sleep finally got the best of me.

I was dreaming, and it was quite pleasant. Yet, I couldn't say what it was about, only that it involved Neera and me. We were under water, swimming towards the sunken city when I suddenly got caught in a riptide. That never happened to me. I had a nearly supernatural talent for detecting undercurrents. The city faded before me, swallowed by a bright, luminous vortex, sucking me with brutal force towards its gaping maw. Dragged by too strong a current, I failed to escape its grip.

"Neera!" I exclaimed when I vanished into the light without any sign of my mate nearby.

"I'm here. Everything's fine. You were just having a dream," Neera said in a soothing voice.

My eyes snapped open only to see Neera's staring back at me while her palm gently caressed my cheek.

"You're awake!" I whispered, shock, joy, and shame warring within me. "How are you feeling? Are you in pain? Do you—?"

"I'm fine," she said in an amused voice, interrupting me. "Well... I'm different but feeling fine."

A simple glimpse at the window, through which late morning light flooded in, only increased the shame burning in my gut. It had been early evening when Mother left after bathing Neera. I had slept through the evening, the entire night, and most of the morning instead of watching over my mate. I couldn't believe Mother hadn't awakened me when she undoubtedly dropped by this morning.

"I'm so sorry for falling asleep. I—"

"Stop it," Neera said sternly. "You're a person, not a machine. You need rest, too. I don't know how long I was out, but I know it was at least a few days because I remember at least two mornings and nightfalls. And each of those times, you were by my side, caring for me, taking away the pain."

"As is my duty," I argued. "As your mate, and as per your human wedding vows, I pledged to look after you, in sickness and in health."

"And you have. But that pledge also means you have a duty to look after yourself as well. How will you take care of me if you neglect your own health so much that you collapse or become ill?" Neera gently challenged.

I opened and closed my mouth a few times, valid arguments failing me, especially as both Raen and my mother had given me similar earfuls over the past few days.

My mate smiled and caressed my cheek again. "I love

how cherished and protected you make me feel, but you must promise me to also take care of yourself. Because if you fall sick, I will be as distressed—even more so—than you have been about me. Do you really want to put me through such trauma because you're neglecting yourself?"

I scrunched my face, glaring at her for that low blow. "You play dirty," I grumbled.

She grinned shamelessly. "Like you, I vowed to take care of you, for better or for worse, and in sickness and in health. If I have to use underhanded tactics to make sure you take care of yourself, you better believe I will. I like you *a lot*, Echo Doja. And I want to keep you for a very long time."

A wave of warmth and affection swelled in my chest as I drew my mate tightly against me. "And I like you beyond words, Neera Michaels. I'm determined to keep you until my last breath."

She smiled with a world of affection in her now typically Thalan eyes. I doubted she'd even realized she now had a second pair of eyelids in the form of a nictitating membrane, which closed vertically before her eyes a split second before her normal eyelids blinked. Like me, her eyes were now bigger than the standard human size, as were the irises, eating up a larger part of her sclera.

Neera leaned forward and kissed me. I cupped the back of her head and took over, immediately deepening the kiss. Despite that, it wasn't our usual lustful passion that had prompted or fueled it, but the increasing affection that had been steadily building between us. I broke the kiss shortly thereafter and, this time, it was my turn to caress her cheek. The familiar texture of her Thalan skin felt oddly foreign to my touch, my tactile memory still looking for the softness of her formerly human skin.

"How long have you been awake?" I asked, still feeling guilty about falling asleep, although the rest had been much needed. I no longer felt like a zombie.

"Only a couple of minutes before you did. I was a bit disoriented, and my body feels strange," Neera said pensively.

"Unpleasantly strange?" I asked, worry slipping into my voice.

Neera shook her head. "No. It's just different. I mean, I've got scales, webbed fingers, and gills! We need to go swim."

"No," I said in a tone that brooked no argument. "We need to take you to Adva so that she can make sure everything is fine."

"Actually, we need to go to the kitchen because I suddenly got so hungry, I'm tempted to take a bite out of you," Neera countered. "You're looking mighty tasty right now."

As if to reinforce her point, a loud, rumbling sound rose from her stomach.

"Blast! Why didn't you say so immediately?" I asked, disbelievingly while also feeling annoyed with myself for not thinking of it first. "Let's go feed you at once."

I jumped out of bed and circled around to help her up, but Neera got on her feet on her own, looking quite steady. Still, I escorted her out with one arm around her waist for support. Although it shouldn't have surprised me, my heart warmed for my mother when we found a copious meal already waiting for me on the table.

"I'm recognizing Edlyn's handiwork here," Neera said, her stomach rumbling again.

"She's been looking after me so that I could focus on you," I said affectionately.

"I love your mother. She's awesome," she said with a tender smile.

That pleased me beyond words. "She also loves you very much."

I made Neera sit in front of the dishes, lifting the covers of the temperature-controlled plates. She weakly argued when I urged her to eat, feeling guilty about taking my food. Silly female... My mate couldn't begin to understand how much I loved caring for her.

Despite her hunger, Neera took a little longer to eat as she bombarded me with questions about the last four days, pausing from time to time to stare at herself, touch her scales and the new texture of her scaleless skin, or admire her webbed fingers. She almost choked on her seaweed and marinated raw fish salad when the claws of her left hand popped out. She quickly recovered but took a moment to figure out how to retract them.

I just kept a silly grin plastered on my face, thinking how much fun I would have showing her how to master her new abilities. I almost felt guilty for how badly I would further neglect my professional duties. But my mate took precedence over everything else.

As soon as she finished eating, I tried to lure Neera to Adva's clinic, but she insisted on going to have a look at her new appearance in the mirror first. As nervous as it made me to delay getting the healer's confirmation that all was well, I couldn't deny such a natural request. That she had not made a beeline to the hygiene room the minute she'd awakened testified to just how hungry she'd been.

She stood in front of the mirror, admiring herself. To my utter relief, my mate didn't seem turned off by her mutations. I thought she looked beyond stunning. Her scales were a shimmering mix of burnished gold and light bronze that beautifully complemented her yellowish-brown skin. They made her oversized, brownish-green eyes stand out even more. Her waist had narrowed and her legs lengthened.

"You are breathtaking, my mate," I said in all sincerity.

She grinned and nodded, turning this way and that in front of the mirror while examining herself. "I agree. I'm looking like one hot female Thalan," she said smugly.

"Because you are," I said proudly. "But now, let's take you to see Adva."

Despite her obvious reluctance to leave just yet, Neera complied. But as she did so, she pursed her lips into the most irresistible pout that would have put even my mother's performance to shame. My woman was truly becoming a Thalan female. I absolutely loved it!

The minute we stepped out of the house, nearby villagers greeted this stunning new version of my mate with clicks, whistles, waves, and admiring glances that had me puffing out my chest. Although I hadn't left my house in four days, I didn't need anyone to tell me that the entire village had worried over my Neera. Their protectiveness towards my woman only filled my heart further with love for my people.

When we entered the clinic, we found Adva already waiting for us. Neera's bracer had warned her she was awake. She ran all the standard tests, adding a few more I hadn't witnessed before. The absence of tension in the healer or of any apparent discomfort in my mate kept me from starting to panic again.

"The good news is that this first phase of the mutation went perfectly," Adva said while helping Neera sit up at the edge of the medical pod she had been lying in.

"And the bad news?" I asked, worry surging to the fore.

"There is no real bad news, aside from the fact that I can't say for sure if and when the second phase will kick in," she replied with an apologetic look. "Normally, it's two weeks after the first phase. But considering Neera's first phase took four days instead of the standard two, your guess is as good as mine about what will happen when."

"But remaining in this current state of mutation isn't dangerous for her, right?" I insisted.

"Hey, I'm here, you know?" Neera said, looking slightly annoyed.

"Sorry," I said sheepishly, and yet feeling like I just got kicked.

I could be a little overbearing in my excessive need to protect our females. That this involved the female I was falling in love with and to whom I had bound my life only sent my instincts into overdrive. I should let Adva talk directly to Neera and let my woman ask the questions she undoubtedly had before I hogged the whole thing as if it were about me. But blast, that was hard!

Neera smiled sympathetically, a sliver of guilt flashing over her face. "It's okay. But give Adva a chance to give her full prognosis. Then you can unleash the Inquisition."

I scrunched my face and nodded. I didn't know what 'the Inquisition' was. But in this context, and going by the generic definition of the term, I could guess what it entailed. Neera chuckled before turning her enlarged eyes towards the healer in an inquisitive fashion—pun very much intended.

"Like I mentioned, everything is looking good," Adva said to my mate. "You should be able to reach greater depths without negative impacts from the water pressure. You should also no longer have any problems seeing underwater without protective glasses, or breathing without a mask. Your hearing has increased. You should be able to perceive most of our ultrasonic calls. Your tail membranes and your veil are absolutely gorgeous. I cannot wait to see you swimming around as a proper siren."

Neera's face flushed with pleasure and excitement. "I can't wait either to try all of this: the gills, the tail, my new cool eyesight."

"Good!" Adva said, this time taking a serious tone. "You must use all of your new traits *extensively* over the next week or two. But this week is the most important. It is vital that you flex these new muscles before they stiffen and atrophy, which would leave you crippled for life. Only major surgeries could *maybe* revert the damage."

"Ugh, no! We definitely don't want to resort to that," Neera said with a shudder.

"She *will* properly train," I said in a tone that brooked no argument.

Both females chuckled, giving me that insufferable 'Yes, dear' look like I was being a spoiled brat.

"Just don't let him push you too hard," Adva warned. "You will tire quickly in the first couple of days. It's not about intensity, but frequency and duration. You do not need to strain for this. Simply get those new muscles moving. Breathe normally through your gills so they don't seal shut. You don't need to train for hours on end back-to-back. Fifteen minutes every other hour is fine, maybe even better."

"Understood," Neera said, listening carefully to the healer's instructions.

After a few more questions to Adva—obviously including a bunch more from me—we left the clinic on our way to the beach. While Neera's excitement at trying out her new body was contagious, an underlying worry was speaking increasingly loudly at the back of my head.

If Neera followed the standard human mutation pattern, we had four weeks—maybe five—before she moved on to phase three. Would she become a full Sikarian then? Were these my last few weeks with my mate before Triton became poisonous to her?

CHAPTER 11
NEERA

I had a set of gills, scales, and a freaking mermaid's tail! When Dr. Atani first mentioned I might turn into something like her, it had naturally freaked me out. But learning about the Thalans on my way here and then the time spent living with them—short though it had been—had really made me fall in love with this species. And my mutation made me look hot as all hell. I almost wanted to go back just to fawn over my new look in the mirror.

Granted, my long, fin-like ears would take a bit to get used to. Seeing them protrude at the edge of my vision had my head constantly jerking left and right, thinking someone or something was sneaking up on me. Then I'd realize it was just the tips of my ears and feel like an idiot. Their heavier weight, although not uncomfortable, was noticeable.

My skin also felt strange. It clearly no longer matched a human's. When I touched the scaleless areas—mainly my face, neck and part of my stomach, I had the impression of poking a gummy bear. It made no sense considering I'd been rubbing all over Echo for days and never thought of his skin as gelatinous. It was undeniably thicker and slightly rubbery, but dolphin skin had been the comparison that came to mind. Either way, that skin felt warmer, like I was wearing a light jacket even though I couldn't have been more naked.

My bare feet were also rocking the ground. My thicker soles gave zero fucks about the tiny pebbles and other sharp objects that usually stabbed at me with malicious glee whenever I forgot to wear my sandals. Better still, webbed feet were freaking amazing. No more sand stuck between my toes!

However, my ankles felt wonky. The bones changed during my mutation so that, when I activated my tail, I could perfectly align my feet with my legs, like a ballerina on pointe, but without the strain. It would take some getting used to as I constantly felt like my ankles wanted to dislocate themselves or something. It wasn't the case, and I'd get over it in a bit. But right now, it freaked me out.

That said, as much as I itch to get swimming in the great depths of Soigo Reef, Echo forced me to put on the brakes to teach me the basics.

My veil—the flowy fins on each side of my hips that covered my naughty bits—and the tail membranes lining my inner legs were the Devil's invention. The damn things were determined to drive me insane with frustration while threatening to make Echo choke and keel over from laughter.

He had taken me to a discreet section of the beach, past the darter stables. A little nook in the rockface of the mountain, a couple of meters from the water, provided us with some privacy. There, he made me practice stitching and unstitching my membranes to form my tail, and then to loosen my veil.

"Shouldn't I open my veil first before I try to stitch my membranes?" I instinctively asked.

The words no sooner left my lips than I inwardly kicked

myself. Naturally, my fiend of a husband didn't miss the opportunity to tease me.

"As much as I relish the view of your intimate parts, we're here to train, woman. Focus."

I made a face at him, which only made him chuckle.

"You have two pairs of membranes along the inner side of your legs. Can you feel them?" Echo asked.

I nodded then focused on the membranes. They felt like an extension of me, the same way I felt my toes at the end of my feet and my ears at the edges of my face.

"For now, bring your legs tightly together, then try to lift the front membranes only and stitch them together," he said.

I complied and squealed like a schoolgirl when that worked like a charm. Echo's teasing smile seemed to imply that I was celebrating too quickly. But I intended to show him how an awakening human rocked her new body. As expected, he asked me to stitch the membranes in the back next to complete my tail. That part worked just as perfectly, except the front membranes split open, and the two fins forming my veil flopped to the side, leaving my hoo-ha exposed to the falsely scandalized gaze of my husband.

I yelped and instinctively tried to cross my legs. But the membranes binding my legs in the back held firm, making me lose my footing. I cried out again and would have faceplanted had Echo not caught me.

"Jeez!" I exclaimed, willing the back membranes to open so that I could stand normally again.

After making sure I was steady on my feet, Echo let go and took a step back while playfully glaring at me.

"Stop flashing your nudity, woman! I will not succumb to your temptress wiles. We have training to do. You get to seduce me later. Have you no shame? Close that veil!"

I gasped in disbelief. "I didn't do it on purpose!"

"Mmhmm…" Echo said in a dubious tone. "And yet, I'm still not seeing a closed veil."

"Argh! I want to kick your ass so badly right now," I mumbled, while attempting to close my veil.

The wretched thing closed in the back, but not in the front. However, the frontal membranes stitched together. I tried to detach them and close the front veil, but only succeeded in flaunting the goods again, while stitching the back membrane. It felt like my brain had been cross wired as far as handling my tail was concerned. Ever the smart ass, Echo teased me to no end. By the time I finally got the hang of this thing, I was deliberately mooning him whenever he would make a taunting remark.

At long last, I got to jump into the water, but not before almost faceplanting again. I needed to remember to unstitch before I tried walking. Then again, I could always hop to the water, but my wobbly ankles made it a no-no. Restitching after I'd waded in thigh deep proved to be yet another mind-fuck. The water lapping against my legs was throwing off my perception of my membranes, causing a few false starts before my tail was good to go.

And then my wretched husband made me unstitch it!

"We're not going to swim just yet," he said with a shit-eating grin. "First, you must learn to breathe through your gills. We don't want you drowning now, do we?"

"Seriously? How complicated can it be to just breathe?" I asked, annoyed.

"For me? No more complicated than stitching my tail. For you? Well…"

He left the question hanging between us with an obnoxious expression on his stupidly handsome face. I wanted to throw something at him.

"I don't like you too much right now," I grumbled.

"That's fine. You're going to like your gills even less in a minute."

The ominous way in which he said that immediately worried me. He extended a hand towards me. I took it without hesitation and let him lure me down the incline deeper into the water. The steep angle had me shoulders deep after only a few steps.

"The biggest challenge for you will be to rewire your brain so that you switch to your gills underwater, then to your nose in open air. Trying to breathe normal air through your gills burns horribly, with very little result. And I don't need to tell you what inhaling water through your nose feels like."

I shuddered at the thought. Chastised, I carefully followed his instructions.

"First, lower yourself into the water up to your chin, so that it covers your gills. Now, try breathing through your gills only," he added once I complied.

Naturally, my gills completely ignored my wishes, and I kept breathing through my nose.

"What the hell?" I said in annoyance.

Echo gave me that obnoxious I-told-you-so grin that made me want to kick him again. The wretched man was awakening my violent side, even though I'd never act on it. In truth, I didn't actually want to hurt him, but I wanted to take him down a notch. And yeah... okay, I did want to smack him, a little... or throw something at him.

His throaty chuckle seemed to confirm that he knew exactly what thoughts were crossing my mind.

"Next time Raen, Opire, and Ouren gang up on you, you better believe I'll join them," I mumbled.

Totally unfazed, Echo smiled smugly. "You won't be doing much ganging up on me if you can't breathe under water, as that's where they usually pick on me," he deadpanned.

"Gill breathing incoming," I said with defiance.

I pinched my nose with two fingers and closed my mouth before inhaling deeply. For a second, I only felt my throat contracting as no oxygen made its way in, and then my gills burst into action, as if they'd been jump started. It was the oddest feeling, the sensation similar to when the air brushes against the inside of our nostrils as we inhaled, but this time on each side of my neck.

The triumphant grin that began to etch on my face froze moments later when my ear popped as I tried to exhale. My face likely gave away what had just happened because Echo burst out laughing. I was opening my mouth to berate him, but he spoke faster.

"You had the right idea. But spare your ears from painfully popping by breathing out through your mouth or nose until you've got a better control of your gills," he explained, his face quickly losing any teasing edge. "When you inhale, focus on the feeling of your gills expanding and on each muscle involved. This is going to be your biggest challenge: relearning how to breathe. But it is vital that you do. You do not want to start breathing through your nose underwater if you get startled, amused, or scared. That may make you panic and put you in jeopardy."

I nodded, sobering at the serious way he spoke those words. I hadn't thought of that aspect, only assuming that having gills would instantly solve all of my problems. I resumed training, really putting some serious effort into it. After God knew how long, I could finally breathe through my gills without holding my nose, but air still came in both ways. I had to focus on blocking my nasal airway before inhaling for it to work properly. Clearly, it would take a while for this to become instinctive for me.

When Echo called a break, I straightened out of the water and immediately hissed with pain.

"FUCK!" I exclaimed, slapping both my hands on my gills as if to contain the burning sting from them.

Echo cringed, his face taking on a sympathetic expression. "That's the other thing. You want to avoid trying to breathe through your gills in open air. Not only does it hurt, but it won't do much for you."

"No kidding," I said, feeling utterly annoyed. "How will I ever master this thing when I need to rewire my brain every time I go in the water, then switch it up the minute I come out?"

"Practice, I'm afraid," he said in a commiserating voice. "Release your gills, Neera."

My hands instinctively pressed more tightly on my gills, keeping them flattened. I scrunched my face while breathing a few more times through my nose to refamiliarize myself with what I'd done since birth. With much reluctance, I gingerly removed my hands, carefully inhaling while bracing for the burn.

Thankfully, it didn't come... at least not yet.

Echo closed the distance between us and drew me to him. His hands settled on my shoulders and his thumbs gently caressed my gills.

"Do not be discouraged, my Neera. You may not think so right now, but you are doing phenomenally well. This is *a lot* for you to absorb and master. Your body is being almost completely rewired," he said in a soft and encouraging voice. "Infants learn how to crawl, then walk, then run. You're trying to run a marathon when you were just reborn this morning. Patience, my mate. We have our whole lives before us. Do not try to rush through this journey. You will only experience a Thalan birth once. Enjoy it. Savor the discovery of the new wonders you now possess."

I nodded, my shoulders slouching a bit, and my lips pursing into a bit of a pout. "I know. You're right. I'm just eager."

Echo chuckled, a happy and tender expression settling on his face as he stared at mine. He playfully pinched my pouty lip, and I realized then what had triggered his reaction. His mother had encouraged me to be a little pouty with him, without going to extremes. For a reason I couldn't explain, I felt the urge to test that theory and further pursed my lips while taking on a dejected expression.

This time, Echo burst out laughing, and he affectionately wrapped his arms around me, kissing my forehead then my pouty lips. "Now, now, no reason to be so sad. Even though you need a lot more practice, we can still take you for a swim to try out your tail and gills."

I perked up, all playful testing gone. "Really?" I asked, my voice full of hope.

He beamed at me and nodded. "Really. I brought a nose clip for you to make sure you won't accidentally breathe through your nose so that we can take a dive."

"Oh, my God!! You're the best!"

I crushed his lips in a grateful kiss before burying my face in his neck and giving him a tight hug. His chest vibrated as happy, indulgent laughter rose from him. Echo gave me a gentle squeeze then kissed the top of my head.

"My sole purpose is to make you happy, Neera. As long as I can keep you safe, I will always try to grant you your heart's desires."

The solemn way in which he spoke those words almost felt like a pledge. I lifted my head to look at him. The adoration in his gaze wrecked me.

"I'm so grateful I married you. I thought my 'illness' was a curse. But now I see it was instead the blessing that brought me to you."

A powerful emotion crossed Echo's face, making my throat tighten. "As you are to me, my mate. We were destined."

I melted against my husband as he captured my lips in a tender kiss. Although he deepened it, there was none of the burning passion that took us over at night. This was full of hope, tenderness, and the love blossoming between us. Although Kayog had not been able to swear we were a perfect match, I no longer doubted we were.

When Echo released me, we smiled at each other with this weird shyness and slight awkwardness that had us both giggling like teenagers after sharing their very first kiss.

"Let's get you swimming," Echo said, looking slightly embarrassed.

To my pleasant surprise, I didn't dick around stitching my tail, succeeding at my second attempt. Echo helped me adjust the clip on my nose before we dove.

To my relief, we remained near the surface for a good ten minutes. I hated that I still didn't have iridophores to communicate under water, but at the same time, that was another language to learn.

At first, I feared that my gills wouldn't draw enough oxygen into my lungs. It took me no time at all to realize that the impression of lacking air was purely psychological, as proven by my perfect oxygenation levels displayed on my bracer. Thankfully, our earlier practice had gotten me comfortable enough with exhaling through my gills.

Soon enough, we were diving deeper. I assumed we would go visit the darters cave that I hadn't been able to approach last time, but Echo took me further away from the beach, in a more open sea. I could only presume that he didn't want me getting distracted by the pets so that I could instead focus on my body and how it reacted to this new environment.

Being able to see clearly with my eyes open underwater blew my mind. That I managed to maintain my body heat despite the cooling temperatures of the water the further down we went also boggled my mind. My new skin was working its magic. But I suspected I would need a thicker layer of fat between my skin and my muscles to further insulate myself in order to reach even greater depths.

Still, I was a freaking mermaid. My body took to swimming like one with an almost supernatural ease. The speed at which I was zipping through the water was intoxicating. Echo and I began racing, not that I remotely stood a chance. He was quite literally swimming circles around me. Then he pulled me into his embrace, face-to-face, our bodies flush against each other's. I synchronized my movements to his, our tails moving as one through the water in a surreal dance.

I'd never felt so free, so in harmony with the universe, and so crazy about my man. I could have stayed like this forever, but Echo eventually released me. We had been underwater a while, and I could feel the first pangs of hunger manifesting themselves.

Feeling playful, I tagged him before racing towards the village. He grinned and gave chase. Although he could have easily passed me, Echo remained just behind me, tickling my tail. I was having a blast.

When he suddenly rushed ahead, but to the side of me, I veered left, thinking he was trying to cut me off, but noticed too late that he was gesturing for me to turn right. Before I could comply, a strong undercurrent swept me away. In my surprise, I yelped but miraculously didn't inhale any water, although I did swallow some before closing my mouth. I immediately started swimming against the strong current— pretty much in vain—but Echo gestured for me to stop while dashing in my direction.

He caught me, wrapped himself around my body, and forced me to lean back, thus letting the current drag us further away. While this slightly freaked me out, having him by my side, calm and strong, reassured me. The current carried us maybe sixty meters before its strength started waning. Another ten or fifteen meters later, we simply swam out of its grasp.

Holding my hand, Echo led me to the surface. It surprised me to see how far we were from the shore.

"Breathe through your mouth," he warned preemptively as soon as we surfaced.

I smiled and nodded gratefully at the reminder, although I had instinctively done so.

"You got caught in a riptide. Never try to swim against the current. You will exhaust yourself and likely fail," Echo explained. "Try to swim perpendicular to the current to exit it. If it is too strong and there is no debris in sight, lie on your back and ride it. It will usually dissipate after a reasonably short distance. There are certain visual signs that help detect a riptide or undercurrent. I will show them to you later."

"Okay. I had really not noticed anything," I said sheepishly.

"This one was indeed harder to detect. But at least, it wasn't in a cluttered area, near a cliff or large debris. When you are closer to the shore, pay attention to darker areas in the water. They are often signs of a riptide as the current picks up sand and sediments. Those can be really fast and strong and send you crashing into obstacles."

"So, avoid riptides and undercurrents," I said with a nod.

He hesitated before shaking his head. "Undercurrents can actually be great. When we travel over long distances, we usually ride some of the permanent undercurrents to rest a little while getting quickly closer to our destination," Echo explained. "They are also essential to help maintain the balance of heat and nutrients in the water. You just have to be careful not to get caught by surprise, and then remain calm to get out of it if you do."

I nodded again, this time in understanding. "I have to say that, once you caught me, it was rather nice. It almost felt like bobsleighing underwater. I could see myself doing that for fun."

Echo chuckled. "Younglings—and adults as well—do it often for entertainment. We even have games and competitions where you must race each other in the undercurrent to try and catch a small target released within it."

"That sounds like fun," I said with a grin.

"It certainly is. But for now, we need to take you home to rest and eat," Echo said firmly. "Do you feel strong enough to swim back to the beach or should I call Braga?"

I shook my head vigorously. Although I was getting

hungry, this underwater swimming business was way too much fun.

"Let's swim!"

"After you, my mate," Echo said, gesturing towards the island.

CHAPTER 12
NEERA

The return to solid ground took far less time than I had imagined. This new body zipped through the waves like no one's business. I remained in the water, submerged to my shoulders and partially hidden behind Echo before wrapping my veil around my naughty bits. To my relief, it didn't open when I unstitched my tail. My husband chuckled with approval and amusement at my proud expression.

His smile broadened when I dragged him to the waterfall. Echo firmly believed that, sooner than later, I'd get over my obsessive need to rinse off after coming out of the water. He was probably right, but right now, off to shower we went.

The waterfall was a little slice of paradise, the water raining down a cliff of the mountain that surrounded the island shaped like a horseshoe. It fell into a large pond, which trickled down in turn to the ocean. The light grayish-blue rocks framing the pond almost looked like they'd been deliberately sculpted and stacked to form a three-tiered platform where the locals could lounge in-between dips. And all around it, the exotic, pastel-colored trees and vegetation typical to the planet brightened the space.

Although there was almost always someone rinsing or chilling by the waterfall, this place was never crowded, and in fact offered quite a bit of intimacy. Echo led me to one the nooks we'd taken to use whenever we showered here. The water rained gently down without the full force of the waterfall.

In a number of recesses carved directly into the rock, eco-friendly soaps could be found. While the Thalans didn't use them often, I systematically did. It wasn't just a matter of clinging to human habits, but my skin always felt a little oily and not truly clean if I didn't wash with soap.

However, things didn't quite go as usual.

Water and dirt didn't cling to my scales and 'dolphin' skin the same way they used to with my human skin. Whether I merely rinsed off or actually washed using that soap, my skin and scales felt just as clean. I could clearly see why it would eventually feel pointless to bother with soap. Then again, since my mate made it his duty to wash me, I certainly wouldn't complain about him working up a lather before rubbing his hands all over me.

We always got a little frisky, but so did other couples. Even now, a triad—a female with her two lovers—were exchanging kisses and caresses in the pond. They would likely soon retire to one of their houses to take things to the next level.

Pairings on Triton were quite interesting. With the population's focus on reproduction, most unwed females had between two and four partners in a loosely polyamorous committed relationship. It was always entirely the female's choice how many partners she would have and who they would be. Naturally, she usually picked males that got along as some of the triads or quads ended up sharing the same residence. But many females chose to live alone or with the main partner of her harem.

The best—and somewhat surprising part—was the apparent absence of jealousy between the males for having to share her. Their collective objective seemed focused on making her happy. Considering the low number of females in their entire population, these kinds of arrangements made sense.

Such relationships could last a few months, a few years, or in some cases decades. Beyond the genuine affection between them, the main focus was to hopefully procreate. In the luckiest triads, the female would give a child to each of her partners. Finding out that Edlyn was part of a triad had stunned me. Two of her partners lived here on Soigo Reef. Her third partner, and the one she'd been with the longest was Leith, Echo's father. He was scheduled to return to Soigo in about a month from now. I couldn't wait to meet him.

The few that actually found their soulmates normally dissolved their harem to marry, at which point they permanently became monogamous. It was a relatively rare occurrence, with only about five percent of the population officially entering wedlock. No wonder the population considered Echo and I to be blessed that we should have found each other even though we lived in two completely different solar systems.

On a side note, although this wasn't officially a matriarchy, children got their last name from their mothers.

As self-conscious as I had felt in the early days about any sensual display with my husband in public, the Thalans' laidback views on sexuality really helped me loosen my own. That didn't mean going all out in front of everyone, but kissing and light groping performed discreetly were more than acceptable. And right now, ours was intensifying to the point of requiring privacy. Echo picked me up, kissing me even as he carried me like a bride. I no longer minded the knowing smiles that followed us as we made our way home.

To my utter annoyance, one of the villagers—named Zale I believed—came running our way, catching up with us only a few meters from our porch.

"Echo, apologies for bothering you, but we need you at the darter stables. There are complications with Kriti's pregnancy," Zale said.

My irritation immediately melted, giving way to concern.

"Give me a second," Echo replied before turning to me. He carefully put me down on my feet and caressed my hair. "I must go tend to her. Go in and get something to eat. There should be more than enough options in the cooling unit and the tank. I'll return as soon as possible."

"Okay. Good luck," I said.

Echo smiled, kissed my forehead, then hurried to the stables with Zale. I thought of tagging along, but I would likely only get in the way, and now that my lusty haze had faded, my hunger was returning with a vengeance. All that water play really burned through a lot of energy.

I whipped up a cold meal, something we often ate during the day and evenings. Thalans served most of their hot dishes in the morning as breakfast constituted their main meal. They usually only had a second meal in the evening, often comprised of shellfish, a variation of seaweed or kelp salad, and those scary raw fish they chewed in their throats. As there were already five perleens swimming around in the tank, I made enough of the side dishes for Echo.

Despite eating very slowly, by the time I finished and did

the dishes, my man still wasn't back. I made my way to the bathroom to check myself out some more. I was still Neera, but definitely different.

I always loved the color of my eyes. But now, being bigger and the irises larger, they stood out in a way that was both highly feminine and sexy. My forehead hadn't changed as I had not developed the vertical bumps the Thalans possessed, but my hair matched their impermeable one. Although it remained as fine and lustrous as it had always been, my hair's texture felt a little rubbery, almost like a string-sized electrical wire. My new skin looked luminous, and my scales gave the impression I was covered in shimmering gold and light bronze little gems. And my tits! Goodness gracious! Whatever sagginess they'd experienced before belonged to a distant past. It should be illegal for a woman's breasts to be this firm and perky. I freaking loved it! My waist had narrowed, giving me that sinfully hot hour-glass figure that some women got a rib removed to achieve.

The bright patterns on my veil and the tail membranes between my legs were delicate and elegant. You'd think they'd been embroidered with golden thread. My fin-shaped ears would probably take the longest to get used to. But even as that thought was crossing my mind, my ears' newly enhanced sensitivity picked up the soft sound of Echo's feet shuffling on the floor as he approached.

He found me still admiring my new looks in the mirror.

"How is the darter?" I asked.

"Fine. Both the mother and fetus are doing well," he said distractedly while observing me. He slightly frowned, tension stiffening his shoulders as he stepped closer to me. The sliver of worry that settled on his face took me aback. "You are very beautiful, Neera."

I smiled as understanding dawned on me and felt both touched and amused that he thought my new appearance troubled me. "I know. I mean, look at these fabulous boobs!"

He snorted, instantly relaxing, and came to stand behind me. Slipping his hands around my front, he boldly settled his palms over my breasts, giving them a gentle squeeze. He then slid his hands down my side to rest them on my hips, over my veil.

"They *are* spectacular," he concurred before nuzzling my nape.

"I like my scales, too, although they are a little itchy," I said with a pout.

Right on cue, Echo smiled. He truly had a thing for pouty lips.

"Unfortunately, that's normal. They're still growing. It should fade in the next couple of days. They'll be even shinier then. You'll be beyond breathtaking. But if it's really unpleasant, I can ask Adva for some soothing cream that I will apply on you."

I glanced at him over my shoulder and smiled. He was also so damn sweet. "Thank you, but it's not so bad—for now." I turned back to look at my reflection. "I genuinely love my new look. Sure, all these changes are a lot to process and to get used to, but they feel right."

He nodded then kissed one of my pointy ears. "Because they are. You were always meant to be one of us."

Echo's hands moved over my stomach, drawing me closer to him. I leaned back, resting the back of my head on his shoulder. He tightened his hold and gently brushed his lips over my gills, making me shiver, before pursuing a path down to my shoulder where he placed a soft kiss.

I loved the look of our joined reflections in the mirror.

Having struggled my whole life with low self-esteem, I'd never been one to fuss over my appearance. And yet, for the first time, I truly found myself beautiful and thought Echo and I made a stunning couple. I suddenly wondered what our child would look like.

"What is it?" Echo asked. "What thought just crossed your mind?"

I chewed my bottom lip, baffled as to where this impromptu shyness came from. "I was just trying to picture what our child would look like. Would it have your features and my color? The reverse? I mean, are we compatible now that I've mutated more? Are we able to conceive?" I asked timidly.

A powerful emotion filled with longing crossed Echo's features. He turned me around to face him. "Would you like that? Would you want us to have younglings?"

I nodded. "I would love to be a mom. I would like many children, but at least one. If I'm ever so blessed, my kids will *know* that they are very much wanted. They will be loved. I want to be the kind of mother I never had but always wished for."

"And you will be, my mate. You will be," Echo said, kissing me, then giving me a tight hug that almost had me purring. He pulled back and brushed my alien hair out of my face. "I would love offspring, too. As many as we can be blessed with. But to answer your first question, many factors come into play to determine a Thalan's color."

"Between your pink skin and my brown one, I could envision our littles ones could have a nice burgundy or rosy-brown color," I said pensively.

Echo grinned, his face taking on a wistful expression. "That would be lovely." He sighed and caressed my cheek.

"Unfortunately, I don't think we're compatible yet. Like Adva said, the first phase is essentially external changes. If all goes well, you will undergo the second phase in two weeks, and then in three more weeks you'll get all the internal mutations in phase three. This should include changes to your vocal cords so that you can do your siren song."

"As well as making us compatible," I added.

He gave me a tender smile. "As well as making us compatible."

"Well then, we can always practice in the meantime," I said, rubbing my palms over his chest before flicking his nipples with my thumbs.

His breath caught, and his pale eyes darkened. "We most certainly can," he said, his voice dropping down an octave.

He picked me up and carried me to our bed. With my new skin, the mattress felt even more unusual than before. It was soft and cushiony, while still providing proper support. And yet, I couldn't fathom what kind of material it was made of. But like every time such thoughts entered my mind, my husband's demanding mouth reclaimed my entire attention.

Echo was the king of foreplay. Even when I could feel him burning with passion, he reined in his own desires. He always saw to it that I was sated multiple times over before he sought his release—which he also didn't achieve without making sure I tagged along. While I looked forward to all of that, I wanted to do some exploring of my own first. Once Echo got going, he wouldn't relent.

Before he could fully settle on top of me, I pushed on his shoulder. Always extremely attentive to me, he rolled to the side, likely assuming I needed a more comfortable position on the bed. His eyes widened, then he frowned when I forced him onto his back, immediately climbing on top of him. He tried to protest, but I pressed my fingers on his lips.

"You are mine. I want to enjoy my mate," I said before leaning down to kiss him.

Despite his obvious reluctance at being pleasured first, Echo didn't deny me my wish. I loved the way he shivered beneath my touch, the rumbling moans that escaped him when I teased his gills or pinched his nipples. He especially liked when I sucked on the spot right where his jawline connected with his ear. It was highly sensitive. So much in fact that I believed that, with enough persistence, I could make him climax just from that.

But I had a different goal in mind.

Despite his need to please me, Echo would only submit for so long to me catering to his needs before he would yield to the urge of taking over and giving me chain orgasms. With my lips, tongue, and hands, I explored every muscular curve of his body. As I loved a man's nipples, I lingered a moment to lick and nip at his. I actually put a bit of strength in those nips. While he certainly didn't qualify as a masochist, Echo liked getting his nipples pinched and a little roughed up—within reason.

I may not be able to do this anymore if my teeth sharpen like theirs after phase two or three.

But that was future Neera's problem. For now, hearing my husband hiss with pleasure had me throbbing in all the right places. I pursued my journey down, teasing his navel with my tongue while rubbing my hand down his hips. He didn't need me to speak to know I wanted him to open his veil. I could see it straining to contain his erection.

As soon as it opened, I resumed my downward path, carefully moving his rock-hard shaft to the side so that I could pay homage to his *sithai*. Just remembering how that inconspicuous looking bump on his pelvis drove me insane with pleasure as it vibrated against my clit had moisture pooling between my thighs.

When I finally turned my attention to his cock, Echo emitted a growling moan that resonated directly in my core, making me even wetter. The first time we'd made love, I had felt how unusual his manhood had been, but he hadn't given me a chance to look at it. Lost in a sea of pleasure, I had just enjoyed and not worried about it. Since then, I'd discovered what wonder my man hid behind his veil and that brought me to the highest peaks of ecstasy.

Like humans, Thalans had two testicles, although theirs were smooth, almost like polished stones, instead of wrinkled. The shaft, long and thick, had a single ridge that spiraled along the entire length like a corkscrew. But that was not the only source of extra feels. A bunch of spikes with rounded tips formed a ring below the head.

I gently began stroking him, while my tongue teased and laved his balls. My hand moving along his length systematically stopped below the spikes. They were highly sensitive and would bring him to the edge in no time. But I wanted to make the torture last a little. Echo moaned, his hips moving slightly in counterpoint to my caress.

His hand found its way to the back of my head. But he didn't try to control or accelerate my movements. Instead, he slipped his thumb at the base of my pointy ears and started rubbing the spot slightly above the one I'd been sucking on him. A bolt of pleasure exploded between my thighs. Each back and forth of his thumb nearly felt like he was massaging my clit instead. I had not realized this was an erogenous zone for Thalans in general.

A moan escaped me as I tried to focus on my task. The wretch had naturally found another way to thwart my plans so that he could pleasure me instead. But I would see him fall apart first. Trying to ignore the growing throbbing sensation between my legs and my inner walls contracting with the need to be filled, I accelerated the movement of my hand stroking him. I shifted my attention from his balls to his glans, licking the head and teasing his slit while his breathing sped up, and the sound of his moans grew louder.

When I finally licked his spikes, a half-strangled, half-shouted moan tore out of Echo. He partially sat up, leaning on his forearm to look at me with an almost pained expression. His hand massaging that sweet spot at the back of my ear stopped, fisting my hair instead while he hissed with pleasure. I increased the speed and intensity of my tongue on his spikes until his legs began to shake. Only then did I take him deep in my mouth. He threw his head back, crying out unintelligible words in Sikarian while I bobbed over him, my hand working him in a frenzy.

Moments later, he fell apart with a savage growl, his hand fisting my hair tightening further, giving my scalp a nice sting. The unique taste of his seed exploded on my tongue, vaguely reminding me of salty caramel, but not as sweet. I looked up at his face, his expression of pure bliss messing me up inside. My man was freaking stunning.

Echo was still riding his high when he took over. To my surprise, rather than putting me on my back, he made me lie face down on the bed. He brushed my hair aside, then his lips zeroed in on every sensitive spot on my body, especially those I didn't even know existed. I'd always been a sucker for kisses and caresses along my nape and the crook of my neck.

However, on top of enhancing that, my mutation had

apparently given birth to new Thalan-specific spots that Echo masterfully exploited. The most sensitive one was the crease right behind the upper edge of my veils on my hips. I nearly climaxed when, while stimulating those sensitive areas, my man's sharp teeth bit my right butt cheek. My legs shook, and I cried out, aching to be filled.

He finally turned me onto my back, but only to pursue this exquisite torture. Except this time, Echo no longer hesitated nipping at me, now that my skin was more resistant. He even gently raked his claws on my scales. When he first settled on top of me, I thought he was at long last going to give me what I wanted. But he didn't join with me, making me see stars instead with his *sithai*. Before I could fully come down, his mouth on my clit and his fingers moving inside of me had me cresting again. However, it was him carefully clawing the tail membranes between my legs that sent me over the edge.

My orgasm was so brutal I thought my spine would split in half. I was still shaking when Echo began inserting himself inside of me. My constricting inner walls all but greedily sucked him in with each contraction. His ridge and spikes as he thrust increasingly faster and harder inside of me soon had me drowning in a tsunami of pleasure. I was writhing beneath him while he pounded into me, begging for more even as my mind threatened to fracture. His *sithai* joining the fray destroyed me.

My throat hurt I cried out so loudly when my orgasm slammed into me. I nearly bucked Echo off me when I threw my head back and arched my back. He tightened his hold around me, grinding his sithai against my engorged clitoris and sucking on my gills to keep me flying a while longer.

As I began to reconnect with reality, he turned me to my side, settling behind me, and ramming himself home in one powerful thrust. A throaty moan rose from my throat as Echo resumed making love to me with an all-consuming passion. His fingers rubbing my little nub while his mouth kissed and nipped at my nape had me flying high again in short order.

He made me change positions twice more—once on all fours, and then once again on my back. That ultimate time, he finally joined his voice to mine. Slamming himself home, he held my hips with bruising force while his seed shot out into me. Head thrown back, his face constricted by ecstasy, he uttered incomprehensible words in Sikarian between hissy moans.

He collapsed next to me, drawing me close, our bodies still shaken by the throes of passion. I held on tightly to him, feeling loved, cherished, and fulfilled beyond my wildest hopes and dreams.

CHAPTER 13
ECHO

The next morning, while Neera was using the hygiene room, I seized the opportunity to refresh the mattress. After removing the blankets and pillow covers, I picked up the watering can and started pouring water over both the mattress and pillows, making sure they got enough without getting fully soaked.

My mate walked back in the room just as I was pouring the last few drops. She froze and eyed me as if I'd gone insane.

"What are you doing?!"

"Hydrating our bed," I said, instantly amused. I'd suspected she didn't know how it worked and secretly hoped to prompt this specific reaction from her.

"What do you mean by 'hydrating' our bed? That's going to cause mold!"

"Not at all. That's going to prevent it and our pillows from hardening and eventually dying," I said, matter-of-factly.

Neera froze, her gaze moving from my face to the bed.

She stared at it intensely while my words hung between us, slowly sinking in.

"Dying?" she asked in a shocked, disbelieving voice. "Dying as in our mattress and pillows are alive?"

It took every ounce of my willpower not to burst out laughing at her horrified expression. "To the extent that they feed and grow—although these ones are already mature—and eventually die, then yes, they are alive."

"Oh, my God! We've been sleeping and having sex on live creatures?" Neera shouted.

This time, I couldn't hold it and gave into laughter while my mate glared at me in shocked outrage.

"It's not funny!"

"Oh, my love, it most certainly is. If you could only see your face," I said between two bouts of laughter. "They are alive but not sentient. They're the simplest form of multi-cellular living organism. They have no central nervous system, digestive system, circulatory system, or even organs. They have as much thought capacity as the leaves of a plant. Sleeping on them is no different than sitting or lying on grass, aside from the fact that these are far more comfortable."

I chuckled again at the way Neera eyed the mattress and pillows suspiciously, her unease not yet dissipated.

"Then what the heck are they?" she asked.

"They're a special type of sea sponge that acts more like a plant than an animal. It merely requires a bit of sunlight, water, and sodium to thrive. Since Soigo is surrounded by freshwater, it doesn't get enough salt from the water we shed when we lie in bed after a swim."

Her face brightened with understanding. "That's why you were so dismissive every time I told you we were still too wet to get in bed!"

I nodded with a smile. "Yes. We have the vacuum at the entrance to remove the sand from our feet and the excess water so we don't mess the entire house. But we want the remaining water to go to the sponge. It will absorb any water in the blankets and pillow covers as well. Since it's like a plant, there's no waste to clean after it, you just need to water it regularly and change the blankets weekly."

"Fine, fair enough. But it's still weird to water your mattress," she mumbled with that pouty face I adored.

"Come, my mate. Let's go feed you so that we can get Adva's blessing to pursue your training. We have much more to do."

She nodded enthusiastically and followed me in the kitchen.

Neera made some tremendous progress over the following two days. My biggest relief was how comfortable she grew breathing through her gills and effortlessly switching to her nose when she emerged. To me, this constituted the most important lesson to ensure she wouldn't drown. With her leg and back muscles steadily strengthening, my mate was gaining speed while swimming underwater, even starting to try some jumps out of the water. She couldn't build enough momentum yet to do serious aerial acrobatics, but it was just a matter of time.

We spent a lot of time on her swimming techniques to make her more efficient while expending the least effort and energy. Eventually, I would take her on a long journey across the ocean to one of our other cities. We also practiced identifying riptides and undercurrents as well as both riding and escaping them.

Eating underwater proved a little more challenging for Neera. Beyond the fact that she didn't like the idea she was swallowing poopy-pee water along with whatever she was chewing, she felt that between the water and her not being able to use her nose, the food was tasteless. It wasn't, but the flavor was undoubtedly lessened. Since my mate liked her spices, the seaweeds and shellfish I had her sample felt even more plain to her.

Thankfully, she played along, and didn't make a fuss eating pretty much everything I indicated she should try. This tremendously helped keep up her energy levels without us having to constantly go back home to eat. Beyond the fact that my woman was greatly exerting herself during training, her body needed a whole lot more fuel to perform the modifications her evolution required.

The third day, Neera woke up coughing and repeatedly clearing her throat. As was my wont, I immediately imagined the worst. I was ready to drag her to Adva's private home since it was still a little too early for her to already be at work when a comment Neera made stopped me dead in my tracks.

"I don't have a cold, but it feels like I swallowed a bucket of glass shards. It's like someone used sandpaper on the entire length of my throat," Neera said, sounding miserable.

I froze and eyed her intensely, a suspicion blossoming in my mind. "Does it hurt more when you breathe or when you swallow."

She appeared taken aback at first by my question then paused to evaluate it. She first inhaled deeply, seeming totally unfazed by it. My mate then swallowed, her face immediately constricting in pain.

All tension left me, and I gave her a commiserating smile. "You're not sick, my love. I believe your throat hurts because you're teething."

Neera blinked, her mind appearing to go blank for a

second before horror slowly descended on her features. "What the fuck!"

I bellowed with laughter as she ran back inside the hygiene room. Leaning forward over the counter, she opened her mouth wide to try and see her esophageal teeth. I followed her in.

"You can't see them, sweetling," I said, amusement filling my voice. "They are much too far down your throat for that. And even if you could, there's nothing to see for now. It hurts because they are preparing to poke out."

Neera closed her mouth, straightened, and continued to glare at her throat through the mirror. "Well, throat teeth or not, I still have no intention of eating those raw perleens with scales, skin, and bones."

Her mulish expression made me chuckle. "Well, that's going to be a non-issue for the next few days, maybe even the entire next week. Your esophagus is going to be very sensitive and raw until your teeth are fully formed. That means a fully liquid diet for you in the foreseeable future."

My heart constricted for my mate at her crestfallen expression. Neera loved good food and had a very healthy appetite. Since her arrival, she had started nicely filling out from her previously far too skinny body. Not being able to enjoy proper food would make her miserable enough. But with all the training we were doing, my woman was burning through her reserves in a blink. Seeing how grumpy she got once she was too hungry, the next few days would be quite entertaining.

"Yay," Neera said with a dejected expression before coughing again.

"That said, once you're back to a normal diet, I'm afraid you will *have* to eat those raw, bony fishes," I said in an apologetic tone. "You have to use your esophageal teeth to erode them so that they don't overgrow."

Neera frowned. "What do you mean?"

"Our esophageal teeth grow continuously throughout our lives. They're similar to those of Earth's beavers. Regular use helps trim them down. They are made of a softer dentine, which wears out faster than the enamel that covers our mouth teeth. So, you don't need a lot of work to erode them, but not doing it will become hazardous for you. You will quite literally stab yourself from within."

My poor mate gave me another horrified look. This morning truly wasn't her day.

"I mean, worst case scenario, you could eat corals," I offered, gleefully bracing for another outraged reaction. "You can swallow small chunks whole, and your teeth will grind them to a fine pulp."

"If you're trying to traumatize me, you're doing a fantastic job of it," Neera grumbled, glaring at me.

I held back a chuckle and gave her a sheepish look. "Actually, my previous comments weren't meant to traumatize you, this next one neither, but I fear it will."

"What?" she asked suspiciously, crossing her arms over her chest with defiance.

"We should probably start including ubrils in your diet for the next few weeks."

Right on cue, Neera lost it.

"Are you freaking mad?! I'm not eating finned maggots! Why would you even suggest that? It's not funny!"

"I know, it's not," I said while failing miserably to hide how badly I wanted to laugh. "Ubrils possess certain toxins that help prevent lymphocystis and kill other bacteria our younglings often catch while their scales are forming and their skins thickening. Lymphocystis is very painful and causes shiny, wart-looking, white bumps on the skin. You really don't want that."

I suddenly felt guilty at my mate's expression. She looked seriously nauseated at the prospect of eating ubrils.

"Surely there's a vaccine or some alternative medication to prevent it?" Neera asked, her voice full of hope.

I hesitated before nodding. "Yes, there is. But ubrils are more natural and far more efficient."

"I don't care. Eating maggots is a hard pass for me. You guys can stock me full of medication," Neera said with a stubborn expression.

"Fine, if you insist," I conceded. "But for now, let's take you to see Adva. She should be arriving at the clinic about now. We need to check if we should give you the same diet we give our younglings when they're teething."

"This is so going to suck," Neera said, clearing her aching throat before pushing out her plump bottom lip in that delightful pout I loved so much.

Unable to resist, I chuckled as I drew her in my embrace, gently nipped at the lip before kissing her.

"We'll figure something out so it's not so bad. Come, love," I said, leading her out of the house by the hand.

Despite all the uncertainties that still surrounded my mate and our future, I was happy... truly happy. Neera exceeded everything I had hoped for and caring for her was filling a burning need the depths of which I had never truly understood until now.

A part of me was already mourning the moment she would finish her transformation and training. I had loved every single one of those instants, from the laughter to the panic she'd harm herself, and from her stumbling first attempts to seeing her grow into her true self and becoming the Thalan she always should have been. Would she even need me anymore once she fully came into her own?

The beach bustled with activity from all the people who had gone out to get fresh catches, sea greens, or fruits and vegetables from our farms for the morning meal. While our people possessed currency, it was rarely used for common foods that were usually shared. Morning meal fishing and harvesting was usually a community effort. We pooled everything, and each individual took the quantity they needed from what was gathered. Those who had not participated could either pay for some fresh produce or merely compensate by helping out the following day.

The villagers paid a tax that served to compensate our farmers for the common roots, fruits, and meats they always provided for breakfast. More specialized produce, meats, and cuts were bought individually directly from the farmer.

This morning, I had meant to catch up with Jorah, our expert fisher when it came to rare seafoods. I had planned on preparing a special meal for Neera, each dish linked to an important part of our history or a folkloric anecdote about Soigo Reef and its sunken city. As I wouldn't be able to tell her about those tales during our visit tomorrow—assuming Adva gave us her blessing to go so far below—I had wanted to do it now. But Neera's throat quite literally kicked that plan in the teeth.

We entered the clinic to find Adva still lighting up the place.

"Well, well. Someone was eager to see me," the healer said, sounding amused as she continued to fire up her machines.

"Actually, it's more like someone is eager to know what

kind of liquid diet she'll be doomed to and for how long," I said teasingly.

Adva's eyes widened as her head jerked towards my mate. "You're teething?"

Neera scrunched her face in the most adorable air of annoyance. "You guys make me sound like I'm a toothless infant still sucking on my thumb," she grumbled.

I felt terrible about laughing again, Adva joining me with a chuckle, but my woman was so incredibly cute. A part of me also suspected that she held no real anger behind that apparent annoyance. I increasingly believed that Neera was on to my weakness for a pouty brat and was catering to my addiction—not that I minded in the least.

"I can see why you would feel that way," Adva said in a sympathetic voice. "However, Thalans teeth twice, first their mouth teeth, then their esophageal teeth when they're about four years of age. But let's check what's specifically happening with you. Let's start by scanning you, and then we'll do an endoscopy."

"Are you serious?" Neera asked, her face miserable as her shoulders slouched.

"Oh, don't worry. It won't be so bad," Adva said reassuringly.

"That camera tube hurts like hell, and my throat is already super sore and tender," Neera said. This time, there was no playful poutiness but sincere concern on her part.

"Not *our* endoscopes," Adva said in a gentle, almost maternal voice. "First, I will numb your throat and esophagus to spare you any pain. And second, our technology is quite advanced and adapted to comfortably perform this procedure in fingerlings whose throats are far smaller than yours. I promise, you will barely feel a thing."

Those words appeared to appease my mate, especially the fact that our little ones could handle it. I rubbed Neera's back in a comforting gesture before coaxing her into lying down in the medical pod. After finishing the standard scans she'd been regularly performing on my mate since her arrival on Triton, Adva made her sit at the edge of the pod.

The healer poured a clear liquid with a slightly pinkish hue in a cup. It brought a smile to my face as I remembered Mother taking me to the healer as a young boy with my throat aching and throbbing. The liquid, slightly sweet and fruity, had provided me with instant relief. She extended the cup to my mate who took it. Neera eyed it suspiciously before taking a timid sip. Her eyes instantly widened with pleasant surprise, and she gulped down the remainder of its contents.

"Oh wow!" Neera said, rubbing her throat and part of her chest. "This thing is like magic!"

Adva lifted her chin proudly, a smug grin settling on her face as she finished setting up the endoscope. "I told you I'd take good care of you."

"You did," Neera conceded with a sheepish expression.

"I don't have much of a choice, anyway. Your husband over there would probably go crazy on me if I caused you any pain," the healer added, casting a taunting glance my way.

My scales darkened to be thus called out. I couldn't even think of a proper comeback. While I was indeed rabidly protective of my mate, I couldn't see myself ever going crazy on one of our females. I contented myself with mumbling something unintelligible.

Neera immediately tensed when Adva asked her to lie down on her side. Despite her worry, seeing how narrow the endoscope actually was went a long way into helping her relax a little. Still, I stood behind my mate, holding one of her hands while gently caressing her hair.

As soon as Adva activated the endoscope's camera, the giant screen in front of us lit up. The strangest emotion took over me as I watched the camera go down Neera's throat, displaying the first images of her swollen esophagus, and the little bumps beneath the inflamed tissue indicating the location of the growing teeth, a handful of them actually poking their sharp heads through it as they began to pierce it.

While Neera seemed slightly traumatized, a wave of love and longing washed through me. I'd always expected that the first time I'd been standing next to someone getting their teething gastroscopy would be for my child. Now, I could only pray that the next time I witnessed this, it would be with Neera by my side, with both of us reassuring our burgundy scaled daughter. By the gentle smile Adva gave me, my face had likely betrayed what hopeful thoughts flowed through my mind.

"It's looking very nice and healthy," the healer said to my mate in a happy voice. "You're definitely on a liquid diet for at least the next three to four days but likely a whole week. Let's do another endoscopy in the morning to see how your teeth are growing. Then we'll have a better idea what type of timeline we're looking at."

Despite calmly nodding, Neera was clearly dejected. She wasn't fond of the whole esophageal teeth concept. It was strange to me that the one essentially invisible mutation she'd undergone so far would be the one she cringed about. I would have thought scales, rubbery skin, finned ears, and the nictitating membrane of her eyes would have bothered her as they utterly changed her human aesthetic. But no. The growing teeth hidden in her throat was the one making her feel like a monster.

"While we're at it, what do you say we take a peek at your vocal cords?" Adva asked in an upbeat tone, clearly trying to cheer up my mate. "Normally, I'd do a laryngoscopy for it. But I doubt you want me sticking a tube through your nose."

Neera's expression made no mystery she was indeed not onboard with that idea.

"I can have a quick, superficial look at them while I'm pulling out the endoscope," the healer added.

My mate carefully nodded her assent as the tube in her throat made it impossible for her to speak. I cast a grateful smile at Adva who responded with a wink.

The camera moved up to Neera's throat before bending towards her trachea. It didn't travel lower, only giving us a view of my mate's vocal cords.

"Wow, they are evolving, too!" Adva said enthusiastically before pulling the endoscope out. "You're going to get your siren voice much sooner than I expected. I cannot wait to hear how you'll sound!"

Neera perked up as I helped her sit at the edge of the medical pod. "What does that mean exactly? Am I going to be able to sing with the same kind of haunting voices you guys have?"

Adva and I both nodded.

"With practice, you will literally be able to hypnotize and lure any sentient being merely with your voice," I said smugly. "You will be able to attain pitches and frequencies well-beyond the human range."

"Oh, is that when I'll be able to do echolocation?" Neera asked, her excitement growing another notch.

Adva shook her head with an apologetic expression. "Not

exactly. While both abilities can be combined, your ultrasonic pulses come from your head. You haven't formed your dome yet—the bumps that we have on our foreheads. It works in a similar fashion to the melon of Earth's dolphins."

"The melon?" Neera asked, looking slightly confused.

"The prominent forehead of your dolphins is called the melon," I explained. "It contains fatty tissues and fluids that allow them to form ultrasounds. Ours are of a much smaller scale but just as powerful... more even."

Neera stared at the bumps on my forehead while absent-mindedly touching her own smooth and flat forehead. "When will I get that?"

"This should definitely be a phase two mutation," Adva said. "It normally involves a lot of cerebral and dermal changes, like your iridophores and bioluminescence. Getting your domes will also likely be very painful and require strumming. Take heart. You're progressing extremely well right now. I suspect that in a week, or about ten days from now, you should get a large chunk of what you're still missing. The final internal changes should take place in the third phase."

"Sounds good," Neera said with a smile.

"For now, let me prepare you a bottle of daqeel—that liquid I made you drink—to help numb your teething pain," Adva said, moving towards her cooling units. She picked up a tiny cup and showed it to us. "You will use this little cup and fill it up to the top line. Take it as needed, but do not drink more than one cup every three hours. If the pain and discomfort returns within three hours of taking daqeel, come see me."

"Understood," I replied in my mate's stead, which earned me an amused look from Neera.

"As for food, let me put together a list of what you're allowed to consume for the time being," Adva continued.

Working swiftly, the healer filled a tall bottle with daqeel, enough to last Neera a full week drinking every three hours on the dot. She then typed up a list of liquid meals, even adding a link to the recipes for some of them, before sending us on our way. Hand in hand with my mate, I took her home to prepare the tastiest option for her.

CHAPTER 14
NEERA

The next few days sucked the big one. Since arriving on Triton, I'd regained a more than healthy appetite, further fueled by the amount of exertion all this swimming involved. I didn't have much of a sweet tooth, but I loved good food. I liked the various textures and flavors, spices and aromas. And Thalan cuisine had opened me to a whole new world of gastronomic delights. But now, I couldn't eat anything.

Fucking throat teeth... That liquid diet could go kick rocks with flip-flops.

To be fair, the shakes and smoothies Echo made for me were quite good, but they couldn't remotely compare to the awesome dishes he usually made for me. At least, they went down without a hitch and the daqeel Adva gave me numbed the achiness. But my throat still felt weird. Despite knowing it was all in my mind, it felt like it had doubled in size and that alien teeth were crawling up and down inside.

Those damn teeth bothered me to no end. Every time I closed my eyes, images flashed before me where I would open my mouth wide, revealing a monstrous maw filled with needle teeth like those giant sand worms in an old sci-fi literary classic.

I hated that I was constantly in a foul mood lately. Echo certainly didn't deserve it. In his shoes, I would have kicked my grumpy ass out of the house and forbidden me to return until I'd regained a sunnier disposition. I couldn't tell if teething or the liquid diet was to blame—probably a combination of both. I'd recently shown a propensity to get hangry.

Tiring easily didn't help either. Just when I would finally get into a cheery mood about something, I'd get smacked right between the eyes with a savage sleep hammer that demanded I go nap right the fuck now. At first, Echo would take me back home to rest, but after the first couple of days, he made me sleep underwater. Surprisingly, he requested I do so vertically, like some whales do. According to him, it wasn't to quickly go back to the surface for air if needed—as was the case with the whales—but so that, should a predator show up, it would be easier for me to switch to any direction to flee.

Apparently, safe practices demanded you keep one eye open when sleeping underwater in an open space to see predators approach. Ideally, this would be with a group of three or more people with their backs to each other in order for everyone to watch a different area. I'd heard that dolphins did that. Thankfully, Echo spared me that—for the time being—since we were in a safe area, and he was watching over me.

Adva reassured me that there was nothing wrong with me, just my mutation taking its toll. I needed to relax, go with the flow, and not push myself so hard. That was easier said than done. The past few weeks had finally given me a taste of a happy life and it felt like it was slipping away from me, like I was reverting back to the constantly sick and weak girl I had been back on Earth. I simply couldn't seem to get out of my own head.

My iridophores—and ability to see them—finally activating did wonders to lift my spirit. Sadly, that too ended up being short-lived. I had known from the start that it would be a challenging skill to master. But in my now trademark excessive eagerness, I dove headfirst, trying to run before I could crawl, and hit a wall. Reflecting the light a certain way with the iridophore cells of my scales wasn't complicated. But memorizing the alphabet and the symbols proved a lot more arduous.

This light-based 'secret' language worked a lot like sign language. We didn't make full sentences with complete words and elaborate grammar. We communicated concepts. For example, if I wanted to say "I want to stuff my face until my belly explodes" I'd simply sign "I desire eat big." And if I wanted to eat something specific, like Edlyn's seymiak, then I'd spell out that word.

The additional problem was that if the person talking to you was slightly turned, you might not see the full sign correctly and therefore misinterpret their meaning. Echo said that with experience, you eventually compensated, the same way our brains did when we read something with words or letters missing or inverted and still clearly understood it.

I'd been diligently trying to learn and memorize everything. While Echo tried to catch up on the work he'd been neglecting since my arrival, I would hang out with him and the boys, casually training and also learning their trade.

While Echo had gone to fetch Yoni, I approached Ouren and Opire who were each grooming a peridorn of their own. Since my iridophore speech was still limited, I threw at them a variety of basic sentences while treading water.

When I said the water was warm, they both smiled, Ouren replying he loved it. When I said it was a beautiful day, Opire nodded and replied to enjoy it because there was a storm forecast later this week. As I didn't understand 'storm' he had to spell it for me. When I said I wanted to swim, the couple froze, their faces taking on an uncertain expression. Opire asked me to repeat. I complied, which earned me strange looks laced with confusion.

"I do not believe you're signing correctly," Opire said carefully. "What are you actually trying to say?"

"I'm saying 'I want to swim'," I replied.

"Ooooh!" both males said simultaneously, looking relieved.

"That's not what you were saying, dear," Ouren said in an amused tone.

"What was I saying?" I asked, bracing for it.

"You were saying 'I want to shit'," Ouren said with a chuckle.

My jaw dropped, and my eyes nearly popped out of my head while the two knuckleheads burst out laughing. I splashed water at them while glaring—which did nothing to quell their hilarity.

"So, how was I supposed to say it?" I grumbled.

Both males displayed the phrase by reflecting light on their chests. I stiffened, giving them a 'What the fuck?' look when they displayed the exact same thing I had.

"Is this a joke?" I asked. The sincerity of the confusion on their faces threw me. "You just showed me the exact same thing I did."

This time they recoiled and looked at me as if I'd eaten funky mushrooms or something.

"It wasn't the same thing," Opire replied. "The signs for

'swim' and 'shit' are very close but not the same. Watch carefully. This is 'I want to swim.'" He displayed the sign I'd done. "And this is 'I want to shit.'"

When he displayed the exact same thing, my foul mood came back with a vengeance as annoyance soared within me.

"You just showed me the same damn thing twice! This is not funny!" I snapped. "It's hard enough learning this shit without you guys making fun of me and confusing me even more."

The words no sooner passed my lips than I felt horrible. They didn't deserve to have me lashing out of them for what they probably deemed an inoffensive joke. However, their genuinely crestfallen and baffled expression made no sense to me.

"Neera," Ouren said carefully, as if addressing a frightened creature about to bolt, "we are *not* making fun of you. I *swear* we have just shown you two *different* signs."

As I opened my mouth to argue, Echo emerged from the depths with Yoni in tow. His jovial smile faded as he instantly sensed the tension.

"What's going on?" Echo asked.

Opire gave his boss an apologetic look. "Neera is practicing iridophore signing, but—"

"What does this sign mean to you?" I asked Echo, interrupting Opire.

As soon as I made the sign, my heart sank at Echo's shocked expression.

"I don't think that's the sign you intended," Echo said hesitantly. "What are you trying to say?"

The horrible déjà vu made my throat constrict and my eyes prick. "How would you sign 'I want to swim?'" I asked, forcing myself to speak in a controlled voice.

Echo's face lit up with understanding and a soft smile appeared on his beautiful face. "Ah yes, I see the confusion. The signs are very close, so it's an understandable mistake. Here is how you would say it."

This time, tears burst from my eyes. I wasn't crazy. They were all showing me the same thing. Echo wouldn't tease me like this. And yet... I had to be broken... There had to be...

"Neera! What's wrong?" Echo asked, swimming towards me, while Ouren and Opire looked distressed by my reaction.

"It's the same thing! You're all showing me the same damn thing!"

"No, my love," Echo said in a soothing voice. "Please, don't cry. Come, we're going to sort it out."

Slipping a protective arm around me, Echo led me to the shore while we swam at the surface. As soon as we arrived, he walked up the beach then crouched to draw the patterns of two signs.

"This is the sign you've been showing us," he said, pointing at the one on the left. He then indicated the one on the right. "And this is 'I want to swim.'"

I frowned looking at it and pointed at two small elements to the right sign. "You guys never displayed this part," I argued.

"We did," Ouren said, startling me.

I had not realized they'd followed us.

"Here. Do you see them?" Echo asked, displaying the pattern on his chest.

I shook my head, feeling defeated. "I still see the same thing as before."

I hated the quivering of my voice and the pricking in my eyes as emotions threatened to engulf me again.

"That's probably because those two dots are displayed in a

different spectrum. Your eyes probably aren't able to detect them yet," Echo said in a soothing voice. "You're still evolving, my love. Give yourself time. Here, let's try a few more signs to verify that theory."

Sure enough, a couple of tests confirmed that my eyes couldn't see everything just yet. While I had no reason to doubt I would get there, I felt excessively dejected... depressed even.

"Thanks for figuring it out for me. It was driving me insane," I said to Echo with forced enthusiasm.

It didn't fool him *at all*. Echo hated seeing me unhappy in any way. And I hated even more that my stupid mood swings were upsetting him. He would take it as a personal failure. Yet, God knew my husband deserved no blame whatsoever.

"That's what I'm here for, my Neera," he said tenderly, caressing my cheek before placing a gentle kiss on the tip of my nose. "Come on. Let's go back to the peridorns before Yoni convinces the others to wreak havoc."

"Actually, I'm just going to go home and get some rest," I said.

Echo's brow slightly creased, a sliver of worry fleeting through his pale eyes. "I can stay with you if—"

"No! No, don't," I said, interrupting him. "I'm just going to nap. And you've gotten behind a lot on your work with all that babysitting you've been doing with me. I'll be okay."

"If you insist," Echo said with obvious reluctance.

"I do," I said, gently caressing his cheek. I then turned to look at Ouren and Opire standing a short distance off on the side. "I'm sorry I snapped at you guys."

Ouren smiled in a sweet, brotherly fashion, while Opire affectionately winked at me. My stupid throat tightened again. And I forced a carefree smile before turning away to hide the fact that tears were welling up once more in my eyes.

I started walking along the beach. After a few minutes, I changed my mind. Considering how far the peridorn stables were located at the east edge of the bay, it would be too long a walk. I just wanted to go home, curl up in bed, and cry. I got back in the water and swam diagonally towards the main beach where our house was located.

As I approached the shore, I spotted Edlyn's silhouette up ahead emerging from the water. By the way she looked left and right at the beach then back at the water, I instantly knew she was looking for me. Echo had undoubtedly asked his mother to come check up on me. The way her face lit up when she saw me rise out of the water and walk up to the shore only confirmed my suspicions.

"I didn't mean to interrupt your work," I said preemptively as Edlyn closed the distance between us.

She waved a dismissive hand. "No worries. As an aquatic biologist, I have a very flexible schedule. And anyway, you are far more important than any of that."

My throat tightened again, and I averted my eyes as I started walking up the beach with no real destination in mind. Edlyn followed quietly, apparently guessing I needed a moment to collect myself. We cleared the beach, reaching the residential areas in the grassy valley, the wide leaves of the trees surrounding them providing some shade from the warm early afternoon sun. At this hour, with everyone working, there were very few people around.

"What did Echo tell you?" I asked.

She smiled. "Not much. We can't have elaborate conversations with echolocation. He only conveyed that you were distressed. I guessed he wanted me to see if I could help. Can

I help? Maybe you can just tell me what's wrong, and we can try to figure out a way to fix it?"

I heaved a sigh before taking a shuddering breath. "I feel lost, Edlyn. It's like I don't know who I am anymore, or what I am. I feel ill in my skin, like it's mine but not really. I feel like a boat without oars or sails, just being carried by the seas according to the whims of the waves. My future seems so uncertain, as is my place here on Triton."

Edlyn tensed, stopping dead in her tracks. I stopped and turned to face her, taken aback by the deep worry etched on her face.

"Are things not working out with Echo?" Edlyn asked.

"Oh no!! Not at all! Echo is wonderful. Echo is perfect. Beyond perfect, to be honest," I said emphatically. "He's so much better than anything I ever hoped for, or that I probably even deserve."

"Nonsense," Edlyn said, her relief palpable. "You very much deserve him, just like he deserves you. My Echo is crazy about you. We all love you dearly."

"I love you guys, too," I said, my heart filling with affection for her.

She pulled me into her embrace in that maternal way I'd always hungered for. I returned her embrace, melting against her as she gently caressed my hair.

"Oh, my daughter, you are home here. Whatever troubles you, we will sort it out."

I nodded before reluctantly pulling away. She smiled, gently caressed my cheek, then took my hand. I followed as she led me towards the waterfall.

"If all is well with Echo, why are you so uncertain about your future and your place here on Triton?" Edlyn softly asked.

I sighed. "I don't have a purpose. I don't have a career. Back on Earth, my 'illness' kept me from pursuing any serious studies or gaining experience in a professional career. I figured I would study here to make something of myself, but there are no universities. The only school I've seen in Soigo seems focused on agriculture. And the classes are in Sikarian. I mean, I love that Echo is taking such good care of me, but I also need a life of my own. I feel like a burden to Echo, even though he doesn't see it that way."

Edlyn frowned upon hearing those words. "You are not a burden. Have you forgotten what I said when you first arrived on Triton? Our males thrive on caring for us."

"But it shouldn't be at the detriment of his career," I argued. "Echo has been seriously neglecting his pet training. Granted, there are other trainers, but Raen, Opire, and Ouren have been doing a lot of the heavy lifting to compensate. And it's not fair."

"Training you to prevent your new Thalan traits becoming atrophied and leaving you crippled for life is our highest priority," Edlyn countered in a severe tone. "No one would take umbrage over that. The opposite would cause outrage. It would be criminal not to make sure you have the best start in your new life."

"Fair enough," I conceded. "But in the end, it still comes back down to me being entirely dependent on Echo. I have no money and no means of making any. I mean, it's not really that I need anything—at least right now—but it's the fact that I feel trapped and helpless. Echo has been heavily hinting that he could hire me as a trainer. I don't want him doing that out of a misplaced sense of duty."

We reached the waterfall and Edlyn led me to the natural rock formation on the left side that always reminded me of a staircase. We sat there, enjoying the breathtaking view of that natural oasis with the soundtrack of the rushing water in the background.

"Do you like working with Echo?" Edlyn asked.

I hesitated. "Yes, I do," I said at last. "I enjoy it, but I want more. I loved taking care of both the darter and peridorn fledglings. I loved learning about their species, habitats, diets, and how to care for them or mend their injuries. But I want to do that with a greater variety of sea creatures. I don't really see myself focusing my career on training pets. I mean, I don't dismiss the challenge. Each pet is different, and it is an art to be able to bring each of them to their ultimate level despite their individual hurdles to overcome."

Edlyn nodded. "It is a calling, simply not yours. It sounds to me like you are more of a marine veterinarian like Raen. He doesn't normally spend as much time at the stables, but two of Echo's staff have gone to perfect their training, so Raen is helping out temporarily."

"To another city?" I asked, perking up.

Edlyn smiled. "Every type of subject matter you want to learn is available on Triton. However, because we have such a small population, each city usually specializes in a handful of higher education subjects. Being one of the very few natural islands on this planet, and as you accurately surmised, Soigo specializes in agriculture and forestry. People interested in these fields will come here to study. This study travel is one of the many ways single people meet their mates.

"Right, that makes sense," I said.

"For marine veterinary training, there are quite a few cities you could choose from, based on the type of creatures you would want to work with."

"But that would imply leaving Echo," I argued.

"It is not uncommon for couples to part for a few weeks or months to pursue their work or studies," Edlyn replied with a sympathetic expression. "Some partners will return every weekend, either using a shuttle or flying a darter, if the distance allows it. I already know Echo will travel to you during that time."

"That sounds like quite the burden..."

Edlyn waved a dismissive hand. "It's not. It is our way. Leith—Echo's father—used to fly to me every three days when he had moved away to pursue his studies as an architect. Even now, he's away because an important job requires his presence. Now that Echo is old enough to 'look after me' and make sure I don't get into too much trouble, Leith can stay away for longer before he returns to me."

I couldn't help but laugh at the derisive way she said that last sentence.

"Understand Neera that Echo will never hold you back. Not out of duty, but out of genuine desire to see you thrive. It is our way. And as for the language, we have great translation devices that will allow you to function seamlessly. And for programs where there aren't enough students, we have virtual training with truly advanced holographic simulations that you can perform anywhere."

"Wow, that's really good to know!" I said, hope blossoming in my heart.

She tilted her head to the side and gave me an odd look. "And yet, instead of fully rejoicing, you still seem sad. What's truly going on Neera? You can freely talk to me."

"I don't know," I said in all honesty. "I'm an emotional wreck. I constantly feel angry. Everything irritates me, and when I'm not pissed, I want to cry. I don't even know why. I made such a spectacle of myself earlier over something stupid. It's like I'm out of sync with my body, with my mind, with this world... Essentially, with everything."

Edlyn froze, her eyes widening with a mix of hopeful disbelief and cautious wariness. "This sounds like... When was the last time you saw Adva?"

"Two days ago. We're now only testing me every three days. I'm seeing her tomorrow morning. Why?"

"It's just that Thalan females tend to get this emotional when they are pregnant," Edlyn said carefully. "Could you maybe...?"

I shook my head vigorously. "No, that's not possible. I won't be able to conceive until I've completed phase three of the mutation, which will make me compatible with Echo. But now that you mention it, I do tend to be an emotional mess when I get my period, which should be any day..."

This time, it was my turn to freeze. Edlyn gave me a questioning look when my voice trailed off. With the calendar dates on Triton being completely out of sync with Earth's, I performed a quick calculation in my head to confirm the realization that had suddenly struck me.

"I'm late," I whispered. "I should be at least four days into my period."

"Into your what?" Edlyn asked, confused.

I quickly explained to her what a woman's menstrual cycle was, and what it could mean when she was late—especially in my case as I'd always been like clockwork.

Edlyn's face lit up with an excitement I didn't fully want to embrace, but that was also bubbling inside me.

"We're going to see Adva, *right now*!" Edlyn said, all but dragging me after her.

CHAPTER 15
NEERA

A dva looked properly surprised when she saw the both of us barging into her clinic. But the excitement that had wanted to soar within me crashed within moments of me explaining what had brought us here.

"As Edlyn probably told you, Thalan females do not have periods. However, based on Dr. Atani's report, awakening humans have their period up until the beginning of phase three, at which point it ends when your internal organs change," the healer explained. "Let's get you in the medical pod and run some tests, but a pregnancy would truly surprise me."

Despite putting on a brave front, Edlyn was even more devastated than me upon hearing I likely wasn't pregnant. But now, a million different questions filled my mind. Why didn't I get my period? Why couldn't my mutation just follow the normal pattern everyone else's did? What new complications were going to pop up?

I was ready to lose it when the needles of the medical pod finally stopped poking me. They didn't use to bother me much before, but now my patience with everything was beyond thin. The dome of the pod opened, and I sat at the edge, instantly worried by Adva's troubled expression.

"As I expected, there are no apparent signs of a pregnancy. I mean, there is always a possibility that it's in the much too early stages to be detected, but I highly doubt it. While your reproductive organs have begun mutating, they're not yet at a level that I would deem compatible."

"But you have a different theory as to what's wrong with me, don't you?" I challenged.

Adva shifted on her feet, looking a little uncomfortable. "Your various physiological stats are not... what they should be."

"What do you mean?" Edlyn asked.

"It's like Neera is undergoing a mix of phases two and three. There's a lot happening inside of you right now. Frankly, I would expect you to be in a tremendous amount of pain," Adva said, clearly confused.

I shook my head. "There's no pain. I just have this general icky feeling, like something's wrong with my body. And then, on top of that, I'm a freaking emotional mess, with crazy mood swings."

"I see," Adva said.

She cast a look at Edlyn who gave her an almost imperceptible nod before typing something on the interface of her armband.

Adva turned back to me. "Is there—?"

"What was that?" I asked, interrupting her. "Did you just mind-speak to Edlyn? What's going on?"

"Sorry," Adva said with a guilty expression. "It's just a reflex. I didn't mean to hide anything from you. I asked Edlyn to call Echo so that he could be involved in the discussion."

My heart leapt in my chest as a sense of dread washed over me. "Echo? Why? What's wrong?"

"Don't panic, Neera," Adva said in a reassuring tone. "There's nothing wrong per se. But we have to discuss a number of things that Echo will want to hear, and it will be easier to do it with both of you present."

"Things like what?" I insisted with impatience, my temper flaring.

Adva sighed. "The data from these latest tests indicate that you're following a mutation curve matching that of a pure Sikarian, not of a Tritonian."

My blood turned to ice in my veins. "So, I'm going to have to leave Triton?"

Adva shook her head. "Not necessarily. We knew this could happen. Therefore, we've prepared an alternative plan for it. I just want to discuss it with the two of you. In the meantime, I would like to perform a few additional tests while we wait for Echo."

With much reluctance, I submitted to the healer. Yes, I had known this to be a possibility, but I'd buried my head in the sand and held on to magic thinking. Whatever emotional hang ups I'd been dealing with lately, one thing that I didn't waver on was my feelings for Echo. I was crazy about that man. Come Hell or high water, I wasn't leaving him, even if that meant spending the rest of my life with another fucking breathing mask.

Echo arrived shortly thereafter, looking worried, water still dripping from him. Adva didn't seem to mind. Some of the tension bled from his shoulders when he saw me sitting at the edge of the medical pod, alert and seemingly fine. He nodded at his mother as he walked up to me. He tenderly caressed my hair, wrapped his arm around my shoulder, and cast an inquisitive look laced with concern at Adva.

The healer quickly updated him as to the reason for my impromptu visit. The elated expression on his face when she first mentioned pregnancy only to have it crushed moments later broke my heart. Echo's hunger to be a father was almost a living entity in and of itself. I wished Adva hadn't brought it up. I hated seeing such disappointment on his face. But her informing him of the state of my mutation devastated him.

We'd been tiptoeing around that possibly. Well, if I were honest, I'd say we'd been pretending like it wouldn't actually happen. But now we had to face the music.

"Before either of you goes into a panic, I am *not* saying that Neera will *for sure* become a full Sikarian," Adva cautioned. "It's still too early to call. But if her stats continue to follow this curve over the next 72 hours, then you will need to make a decision."

"A decision like what?" I asked.

"The first option is to let your mutation follow its course and allow you to become a full Sikarian," she answered.

"Which means I'll have to leave Triton," I argued.

Adva nodded with an apologetic expression. "Our atmospheric pressure is too low for a pure Sikarian. It would take you right back to the situation you were in on Earth. Which means you would then have to choose between leaving Triton, staying forever in the deepest levels of the sunken city, or wearing a breathing mask every time you want to leave the city or come to the surface."

I shuddered at the thought of reverting to the nightmare I endured on Earth and of being once again stuck with a mask. Living in the sunken city could be an option, although the thought of never seeing the sun again or feeling the caress of a morning breeze on my skin broke my heart.

"The second option would be a special treatment to stall part of your mutation," Adva said.

"What? No! That would leave her crippled!" Echo exclaimed in outrage.

Adva shook her head. "No, it wouldn't. Dr. Atani and I have been extensively looking into the possibility of this scenario. In the end, the challenge is making sure that Neera doesn't breathe in too much oxygen to avoid high toxicity. So, we devised a nanobot treatment that would stall her lungs' and gills' mutation to keep them in their current state, which is perfect for our world."

"That sounds like a pretty good plan," I said, my heart soaring with hope.

"I agree," Edlyn eagerly said. "Then she would be able to finish the rest of her mutation and continue to comfortably live here with us."

"That's right," Adva said with a smile.

Echo shook his head, a deep frown creasing his brow. "I'm not comfortable with that. We should let nature take its course. Neera should be allowed to fully become whatever she was meant to be. Whatever the cost to us."

That hurt. I recoiled and stared at him in disbelief. "So… you want me to leave?" I asked, feeling betrayed.

It was his turn to recoil. "Of course not, my love." He moved in front of me and cupped my face in his hands. "I love you, Neera, and I want the best for you. For the first time in your life, I want you to be whole. Between Triton and Sikaria, we have access to some of the greatest scientific minds of the galaxy. I'm sure we can find a way to stay together without stunting your evolution."

I nodded slowly and wrapped my arms around his waist. He let go of my face and, standing between my parted legs as I still sat at the edge of the medical pod, he pulled me into his embrace. I rested my head on his chest, a million thoughts firing through my mind.

"Well, worst case scenario, like Adva said, I can always live in the sunken city. A lot of your people do it," I said.

"No," Echo said, shaking his head and pulling back to look at me. "That would effectively make you a prisoner for the rest of your life. You'd still be restricted to a few appropriately pressurized areas when not in the water, and be forced to wear a mask the rest of the time. I won't allow that. You've lived your entire life on the surface. You may think living underwater will be no big deal, but as weeks, months, and years go by, it will take its toll. And then you'll see the sunken city for what it has become: a prison."

"Which brings us back to me having to leave Triton… to leave *you*!" I said, confused as to why he didn't seem to get what he was implying.

"I am never going to leave you, Neera." He turned towards Adva. "In the past, a number of Tritonians have successfully relocated to Sikaria. I understand there is a procedure that makes life possible for us there."

"No!" Edlyn whispered, staring at her son with a crestfallen expression that crushed my heart.

Echo turned to look at his mother, guilt and sorrow settling on his face. "I'm sorry, Mother. But I have to do what's right for my mate's welfare."

Edlyn wrapped her arms around her waist, hugging herself. Eyes downcast, she gave him a sharp nod, but I could see her heart breaking at the thought of losing her only son. I didn't want to take him away from her. *I* didn't want to leave her either. Edlyn wasn't just my mother-in-law. She was the mother I had always dreamed of and the best friend I never had. I didn't want to leave Triton.

Before I could say as much, Adva intervened.

"You are correct," the healer said with a nod. "However, it is a far more invasive procedure and way riskier than what we would do to Neera. The success of that procedure on you also isn't guaranteed."

"Neither is the one you're considering doing to my mate," he countered in a severe tone. "You've never performed it on any other human before. Neera would effectively be a test subject in a brand-new experiment. I can't allow that. She's suffered enough."

That argument actually gave me pause. I was indeed the first awakening human to have faced all these difficulties. Could that nanobot treatment mess me up rather than help me?

Adva pursed her lips, clearly disagreeing with my husband's position. "Look, there's no point arguing about any of this now. We still have two or three days to assess how things are evolving with Neera. We can make a decision then. In the meantime, I will contact Dr. Atani to let her know what is happening, and we can take it from there."

We all agreed with the wisdom of her words. With heavy hearts and too many questions unanswered, we left the clinic.

CHAPTER 16
ECHO

How had things devolved so quickly? Only a week ago, life was perfect, the future promising. And now, I had to contemplate the very real prospect of leaving my home-world, my family, my friends, and my entire life to start over on Sikaria with Neera. The devastated look on my mother's face still clawed at my heart. I didn't want to leave her, but what choice did I have?

I was madly in love with my Neera. I couldn't fathom losing her, and I had a sworn duty to protect her, including from my own selfish desires. Her welfare had to come first.

Still, I couldn't deny being worried about the procedure. The possibility of me rejecting the graft to my lungs and gills was a reality I couldn't shy away from. Should that occur, it would leave me with permanent side effects that would impair my breathing and ability to swim. A few Tritonians had successfully done it, but the failure rate was a whopping 14%.

Over the past couple of days, Neera and I had argued a lot about it. I loved that she wanted to protect me, too. However, the Tritonian graft had some history and data that we could assess the risk from. Her nanobot treatment had never been tested before.

"I can almost hear you thinking," Raen's voice said off to my side, startling me.

I finished feeding the ubrils—that would in turn be fed to the young darters—then sealed their enclosure.

"And what am I thinking?" I asked, turning to face him.

"Some nonsense about getting your lungs and gills butchered," he said matter-of-factly.

I recoiled in shock. Raen had always been one to bluntly speak his mind, but he'd never been brutal before. He gestured with his head at the water. I thought he wanted us to dive in, but he sat instead at the edge of the platform of the darter stable, his webbed feet dipping into the water.

I imitated him, settling by his side, like we used to do as juveniles to talk about our great dreams for the future.

"Let Adva use the nanobots on Neera before you rush to get that surgery done," Raen said.

I stared at him in disbelief. As a Tritonian male, he should want me to put the welfare of a female above my own.

"How can you say that? I thought you loved Neera?" I asked.

"I do. And I love you, too. Which is why I'm telling you to stop being an idiot. The nanobot treatment they are planning for Neera is reversible. The graft is not. What if something goes wrong? What if you die or are left permanently crippled by the procedure? Neera will still be a full Sikarian, forced to leave Triton, except she will then do so without you by her side. What will happen to her all alone over there?"

I flinched, that comment striking a major nerve. That

argument had popped up in my mind more times than I wanted to admit, but I kept pushing it away. After all, 86% success rate weren't bad odds. But what if I was indeed in the unlucky 14% that rejected the graft?

"Cousin, no one doubts your devotion in caring for your mate. It is plain for everyone to see. However, protecting your mate also means protecting yourself so that you can be by her side. You should only contemplate things that could jeopardize your own health as a last resort, not your first choice," he said, his voice taking on a passionate edge.

"I hear what you're saying, but the nanobot treatment is experimental," I argued.

"It is low risk! The nanobots will simply stall the mutation in her lungs and gills. If we start seeing any sign of adverse effects, the nanobots are easily removed. We're literally talking a matter of minutes, with no side effects. This is a no-brainer. We may not know that doctor, Atani, but we know Adva. She would *never* suggest this treatment if she even remotely thought it could be harmful to Neera."

I sighed heavily. "I do not challenge your logic. I cannot deny anything that you've said so far. But Neera has suffered so much. It feels selfish to put her at risk just so that our lives can go on here as before, while also depriving her from ever becoming her true self."

"And there's your overthinker self rearing its head again," Raen said in an affectionately teasing tone. "Neera never aspired to become a Sikarian. She just wanted the ability to breathe like everyone else and live a normal life. Being an awakening human was an unexpected surprise she never asked for. I don't know that, given a choice, she ever would have wanted this mutation. But the one thing that I know for sure is that she wants *you* and the life you're building here together. She doesn't have any attachment, emotional or otherwise, to the idea of becoming a full Sikarian. Do you seriously think she would be happy moving away to Sikaria, starting all over, and maybe even alone if your procedure fails?"

My heart ached as much as my brain from all these questions. "She found happiness here when she left Earth. She could do it again on Sikaria."

My words sounded lame and hollow to my own ears even as I spoke them. By the look on Raen's face, he wasn't impressed either.

"She had *no one* on Earth. She found *you* here. Despite how dumb you're acting right now, Neera loves you. Triton is her home, and *we* have become her family. She has a great deal to lose by leaving Triton. Anyway, it's not your decision to make but hers," he added with a dismissive gesture. "And I can already tell you that she will take the treatment."

Feeling defeated, I frowned, and my shoulders slumped. "We'll see when Dr. Atani gets here tomorrow," I said without much conviction.

"We will indeed. But remember that caring for your mate also means supporting her difficult choices, regardless of your personal wishes. You have expressed your thoughts, let it be her decision based on what *she* thinks is right, and not what she thinks *she has to do* to please you. Neera needs to know you will have her back, no matter what."

That, too, made me flinch. In my rabid need to protect her, I had undoubtedly been forcefully vocal about my stance on the matter. I was failing Neera miserably.

"Thank you, Raen. I hate that I needed to hear this," I said dejectedly.

He smiled affectionately. Lifting a hand, he caught me by the nape, drew my face closer to his, and kissed the central dome on my forehead. "Take heart, my brother. All will be well."

With these last words, he pushed off the platform and dove into the water, leaving me with my troubled thoughts.

CHAPTER 17
NEERA

Walking hand in hand with Echo on the beach as we headed towards the water, I savored this fleeting moment of normalcy. Yesterday, Adva had given me permission to start eating more solid food, though nothing too hard or crunchy. That had significantly lifted my mood. I still felt rather icky and ill at ease in my body, but greater pressure seemed to dampen some of my discomfort.

As I was now able to comfortably handle the greater depths required to visit the sunken city, Echo was finally taking me on a guided tour. It sucked that I had not yet developed my mind-speak abilities. It would have made it a lot easier to ask him questions and for him to describe to me what I would see. But we would figure something out.

As Dr. Atani would be here in the morning, I was particularly thrilled to see the sunken city at long last before that meeting. It would certainly help enlighten the decision I would make—although my mind was already pretty much made up.

The sunken city was located a great distance below the

surface, further down than the darter caves. It was partially carved in the rock that supported Soigo Reef, the rest sprawling around it in the same shape as the bay above. It was mesmerizing to get a clearer view of it as we approached.

Multiple organically shaped buildings flowed into each other almost seamlessly. I presumed the desire to let the water flow smoothly over the city explained the mostly round architectural style. Some form of dome covered every building, some pear-shaped. I couldn't tell if the coral reefs interwoven with the city—some sections forming a large garden—had been added after the fact, or if the city had been built around them. Large fields of seaweed and kelp created the illusion of being parks. Above the main city, the rounded windows of individual dwellings protruded all around the rock face, like countless glowing mushrooms.

The entire city reminded me of a giant alien garden, with the same soothing pastel colors from Soigo village. It had a dreamy glow about it that gave the impression that it was pulsating from within. There were no streets per se, but quite a few people could be seen swimming around, going from one building to the next.

I didn't really know what I had expected the sunken city to be. For some ridiculous reason, I'd pictured restaurants with an 'outdoors' terrace, where people sat in the water, mind-speaking, and either catching the small fish that swam by to eat them or grab them out of a holding tank in the center of the table. Obviously, that wasn't the case.

A number of inconspicuous doors allowed the residents to come in and out of the buildings. The number of children and teenagers blew my mind. A small group of them, apparently under the supervision of an adult, were chasing each other around a building strongly reminiscent of a spiraling seashell.

Using his iridophores, Echo succinctly explained that they were having their thirty-minute recreation before their next class.

I loved seeing the little ones. Too few of them came to the surface, and the ones that did usually popped up while Echo and I were at sea training me or his pets. Surprisingly, they all had a fairly similar peachy color, except for the edges of their tail membranes where they seamlessly stitched. According to Echo, the edge color of their membranes indicated the true color their skin and scales would acquire once they matured and became fertile.

The large number and variety of fish that swam around the city shocked me. I would have presumed that they would try to steer clear of their biggest natural predator. But the massive coral reefs interwoven with the city undoubtedly held an irresistible appeal for them.

We made our way to one of the many inconspicuous doors at the base of the largest dome. To my surprise, it turned out to be some kind of energy field to keep the water out. As soon as we arrived in front of it, Echo unstitched his tail, indicating for me to do the same. He then led me through the energy field, which let us in without the slightest resistance.

My knees nearly buckled when we entered the pressurized room. I was used to feeling heavier when I walked out of the water. After all, buoyancy lessened the gravitational force in water compared to the normal force we felt on the ground. But considering the greater pressure at these depths, I'd assumed the buildings would be adjusted to match. Without Echo's prompt reaction catching me, I probably would have crumpled to the floor.

"Neera! Are you all right?" Echo exclaimed, worry filling his voice.

I felt dizzy, like when you were on the verge of hyperventilating. Thankfully, that quickly passed, but I still gave my husband a shocked and confused look.

"Why isn't the pressure here matching that of the water outside?" I asked, shuddering at the thought of the horrible death I could have faced.

"It is just slightly lower and maintained throughout the city so that we can seamlessly come in and out without problem," Echo said, clearly distraught. "It shouldn't have affected you this much. I guess your body isn't quite ready for these depths. I'll make sure to set the pressure to perfectly match outside next time."

"You can do that?" I asked, surprised.

He nodded and showed me a discreet panel near the energy field that served as a door. "It will adjust the pressure in this room to match but it will gradually decrease in this long corridor to match the city's pressure if we do. There's a similar one outside that allows some very minimal tweaks by anyone. Anything more radical would require special clearance."

"Right, that makes sense. You wouldn't want a child messing it up by accident."

He chuckled. "And they certainly are always up to mischief. Are you feeling sick?"

I shook my head and smiled reassuringly. "No, I'm better now. It was just the initial shock that was brutal. We can continue."

It struck me then that I didn't have a single drop of water on me. "Hey! We're both fully dry!" I exclaimed.

Echo smiled smugly. "The energy field keeps *all* water outside. It avoids us having drying stations all over the place."

"Wow, that's super cool. But that seems like a flimsy

protection." I cast a curious look around the circular room we were standing in. Four cylindrical shapes lined the rounded walls of the room, two on each side of the winding corridor in front of us. "If the energy field went down for whatever reason, this entire place would get flooded."

Echo shook his head. "Not at all. There are multiple watertight doors along the entire length of this corridor. The first set is recessed into the walls right here at the entrance of the hallway. There's another set every five meters. Should a breach be detected, they would all automatically close and gradually reopen as the flooded areas were secured and drained."

"Well, that's reassuring," I said, making no effort to hide my relief.

"While most of us simply walk the corridor to the main floor, you could use one of these pressurization lifts instead," Echo said, pointing at the cylindrical shapes. He approached one of them. To my shock, it parted open, revealing a good sized elevator. He waved me inside and the door closed behind us. "As you can see, there are three floors. If ever someone tweaks the pressure in this access room, regardless of the one you select, the cabin will gradually depressurize to match that of the main floor by the time we reach it."

My initial reaction was to wonder why it wouldn't spread the depressurization until we reached our destination floor, but it struck me that if someone else got on at say level one when we were heading to level three, they would get messed up by the modified pressure.

"Let's take a ride," he said enthusiastically.

It was slower than I expected, but then I suspected the depressurization time was the real cause. That couldn't be

I MARRIED A MERMAN

rushed. However, judging by the way Echo frowned, this had taken longer than usual.

"Does this thing track the status of the people inside it?" I asked.

Echo nodded. "The lift monitors the people inside to make sure they are safe."

"So, could it be this slow because it needs to get me up to the proper level without getting hurt?"

His face lit up with understanding. "Yes, that would make sense. It is usually a lot faster. But there's no rush."

He pulled me into his embrace as he spoke those words, and I melted against him. The emotional wreck that I was acted up again. But this time I didn't mind it.

"I'm falling in love with you, Echo," I blurted out.

The joy and deep tenderness that descended over his features as he tightened his hold around me did crazy things to me.

"You had better," he said in a grumbling voice. "Because I'm already there as far as you're concerned. I'm madly in love with you."

I pressed myself harder against him and lifted my face to receive his kiss. It was just the right mix of devotion, passion, and possessiveness to make my toes curl. My fingers sank into the silky strands of his alien hair, fisting it as he tilted his head to the side to deepen the kiss. Just as my girly bits were standing to attention, a soft swishing sound followed by a flood of light snapped us out of the moment.

A series of whistling sounds greeted us as the handful of people standing outside the lift teased us. Where Echo waved them off with an amused but proud grin, my scales turned a dark shade of bronze.

Shortly after my iridophores had become active, my bioluminescent skin cells had also kicked in. With everything else I had to juggle and learn, I'd decided to mostly leave that part alone for now. I only stirred them daily to make sure my ability to eventually control them wouldn't atrophy. That meant I didn't master them enough to shut down my very visible blushing as Echo led me out of the pressurization lift.

But the sight displayed before me kicked all embarrassment to the curb. This place was mesmerizing. At a glance, it resembled a massive, multi-tiered shopping mall. The dome overhead hid nothing of the ocean that surrounded the city, and the walls almost looked organic with an opalescent shimmer to them. What looked like a multitude of stores and businesses lined the walls on each floor, the large central area of the 'mall' had a series of what appeared to be temporary kiosks, as well as an area where buskers could perform.

I couldn't see any escalators or elevators, other than the one we'd just stepped out of. However, large tubes filled with water had been artistically interwoven with the structure, connecting the three visible floors and crossing over each side of the walkways. People could be seen swimming through them, reaching their destination in a heartbeat. The same energy fields at the exits allowed them to step out completely dry.

"This is the Concourse," Echo explained, visibly pleased by my reaction. "Most of our artisans and crafters sell or trade their local wares here. This is also where you will find most of our entertainment venues, such as our theater, which also serves as a concert hall. There are two dance clubs, sports venues, delicacy restaurants, and treats boutiques, to name a few."

Blown away, I followed Echo as he made me visit a number of those places. Knowing my love of food, my husband took me to the treats boutiques. We started first with the ones that specialized in savory treats. They were bite-sized delicacies that usually came in the same format as a chocolate box. This boutique offered seafood-based treats, many of them using 'rare' shellfish, some of which were only found in distant regions of Triton.

The second one mainly used plant-based produce as a foundation, although some also included local seafoods. I'd developed a particular fondness for the one called yaimal. No bigger than dice, they were made out of the equivalent of potatoes and scampi, with local herbs and spices, processed in a way to give them a slightly chewy consistency.

The third one was all sweets. Although they didn't have chocolate—which should be deemed a capital crime—they more than compensated with a variety of other things I had never experienced before.

Unfortunately, in all cases, I had to settle for the softer treats as my throat still wasn't fully cooperating. But I already had my eyes set on a number of goodies I intended to indulge in as soon as possible.

We spent at least a couple of hours in the mall, visiting the different types of shops. Unlike human malls, there weren't tons of clothing, perfume, or make-up shops, since they were of no use to the local population. There were some jewelry and hair adornment shops, a spa, decorations and furniture stores, plenty of waterproof electronics, and stores providing tools and equipment related to water activity.

I could have stayed there much longer, but Echo dragged me to other sectors of the city, namely to give me a quick tour of the various industries operating below. The size of the population took me aback.

"I hadn't realized there were so many people here," I said

as we exited the connecting passage from the water processing plant.

"The majority of Tritonians live underwater," Echo replied. "A lot of our intergalactic trades are related to nautical products or aquatic goods. We also do a lot of environmental and marine biological research. All of it is done underwater. As fingerlings remain mostly in the safety of their respective sunken cities, so do their families."

I nodded as we continued to explore the immense city. The communicating pressurized buildings essentially allowed us to move around and live just like at the surface. Their entire lighting system appeared to be using a form of daylight lamps. Stunning inner gardens made this place a paradise.

When my stomach began to growl, we returned to the mall to have dinner at one of their restaurants.

To my surprise, the one we chose—as well as the others—moved a number of tables outside, near the railing of the walkway. Echo grinned at my baffled expression. He then gestured with his chin at the central area of the Concourse. The temporary kiosks had been removed, and some sort of stage had risen from the floor. All around it, people were gathering, some sitting directly on the floor, while others settled on cushions or portable seats they had brought with them.

"Every other night, there is a performance on the Concourse," Echo explained. "It can be dance, singing, a play, an illusionist, you name it. My favorite ones are interactive crime solving mysteries. The actors tell the tale of crime that was committed, often in the form of an interrogation or a trial. The public gets to choose which questions are asked based on a majority vote. You have to pay attention because you have a very short window to input your vote. And then you try to guess who is the culprit."

"That sounds awesome! I love murder-mystery games!" I said. "Is that what we're getting tonight?"

He shook his head. "No, tonight will be singers and dancers from the Mandra Reef. There will be a crime mystery next week. I'll make sure to bring you back so that we can attend."

I nodded enthusiastically.

The menu looked beyond scrumptious, but my damn throat restricted me to a chowder, although Echo assured me it was almost as good as seymiak... almost. Our food reached our table moments before the performers got on stage.

Once again, one shiver after another coursed through me as I listened to their haunting voices singing in harmony and stared in awe at the mesmerizing and sensual movements of their dancers. The lights of the mall had dimmed, providing an intimate atmosphere, while overhead exotic fish lazily swam outside the dome. It was without a doubt the most romantic and spellbinding moment of my life.

By the time we went home, my mind had been made up. As we lay down in bed, I turned to face Echo. A single look at my face sufficed for him to know we were about to have a serious conversation.

"I could remain in that city. It's absolutely amazing," I said in a soft voice. Echo gave me a pained and troubled look but surprisingly didn't challenge me. "I know you fear it will become like a prison, but if I really need to come to the surface, I'll just wear a breathing mask. And nothing prevents us from visiting another sunken city for a while for a change of scenery. They already maintain a higher pressure down there, closer to Sikaria's. Even if I had to wear a mask, it would be a lighter one."

"That could be an option," Echo said in a non-committal

fashion, although I could sense the underlying reluctance he was trying to quell.

"I'm not leaving Triton, Echo. That's just not an option for me, and not one that I will ever be willing to consider," I said firmly. "Edlyn is now my mother too and the best friend I've never had. Raen has become my pesky little brother—even though he's technically older than me. And Ouren and Opire are the insufferable mischievous cousins you just can't help but love. Soon, I'll have a dad in your father. I've finally found a place to truly call home, with a family that I love and who loves me right back."

"You most certainly are loved, Neera," Echo said, his voice filled with emotion as he gently caressed my hair and then my cheek.

I smiled and turned my face to kiss the palm of his hand. "And above all, I've found you, my impossibly perfect mate. I'm not letting you risk your health or taking you away from your family and loved ones. Especially not when there's a safer solution. Whether or not I'll use the nanobots, that's a decision we can make tomorrow after we've talked to Dr. Atani. But the bottom line is that we're staying here, and I'm not losing you."

Echo silently stared at me for a moment, studying my features as if searching for an answer there. Then he smiled, drawing me into his embrace. "Whatever your decision, as long as we are together, I'll stand by you, my love."

CHAPTER 18
NEERA

Sitting at the edge of the medical pod, I shifted restlessly while staring intently at Dr. Atani. It struck me as an uncanny role reversal that she should be the one wearing a breathing mask this time. Even her gills had been taped down against her skin. I nervously placed my hand in Echo's as we waited for Adva and the Sikarian doctor to finish studying my latest test results.

Dr. Atani turned to face me, her expression harder to read with half of her face hidden by the mask. "Your results confirm what Adva had surmised. You are indeed on a path to becoming a full Sikarian. To be honest, I expected as much. Every awakened human eventually became one of us. Your journey simply happened to be more hectic."

"So, what are my options?" I asked, my hand tightening around Echo's.

"I believe Adva has already talked to you about the nanobot treatment we have devised for you?" Dr. Atani asked, casting a sideways glance at the healer. She nodded, and so did I. "Well, I highly recommend that we proceed with it. I am

99% convinced that there will be no negative impact for you, Neera. And it is completely reversible."

"And that treatment will allow me to continue to live here normally, permanently?" I insisted.

"Yes. It will allow you to breathe normally in this lower atmospheric pressure without harming you," she confirmed.

"How often will she need the treatment?" Echo asked.

"Technically, just once." Dr. Atani said, her eyes softening in a way that implied a smile behind her mask. "We might want to replace the nanobots once every five or ten years. Otherwise, nothing else is required. In truth, I wouldn't be surprised if, after a few years, your lungs and gills permanently remain in their current state, even without the nanobots."

I beamed at the doctor before turning to look at Echo. "You see? There's no reason for us to leave, and I won't be 'trapped' in the sunken city."

Echo nodded. For the first time, he truly seemed relieved and onboard with this course of action. That meant the world to me. I couldn't wait for us to break the good news to Edlyn. The poor female was beside herself with worry we would have to leave.

"You have a solid support system here," Dr. Atani concurred. "There is no reason for us to make you start over on a new world—not that we wouldn't be delighted to have you with us. In truth, I'd love nothing more than to have you on Sikaria. Your unique evolution could potentially help us solve many of our own issues."

I recoiled at that unexpected comment. "How so?"

"The different path taken by your evolution has already helped us identify some Sikarian fetal developmental issues we'd never even been aware of," Dr. Atani said, her voice filling with excitement. "You're essentially like an adult version of our fledglings. Your mutation didn't follow the standard process for awakening humans. You evolved in a manner far closer to the development of our fetuses. Your endocrine system is especially fascinating to us."

She tapped some instructions on the interface of the medical pod then turned the monitor to show us the graph displayed there. It meant absolutely nothing to me.

"Adva has been transferring your data to me to make sure you were doing fine, since I'm an expert in awakening humans," Dr. Atani continued. "This curve shows your hormonal levels over the past week. This tiny peak here is the one that interests us the most. It's from today's blood test and shows the presence of a hormone called CG."

"What's that?" Echo asked.

"It's the Sikarian equivalent of what Earthlings call HCG. That hormone is what human doctors track to determine whether or not a woman is pregnant."

I gasped, my hand flying to my chest, as I stared at the doctor with bulging eyes.

"What are you saying?" Echo asked, his voice barely higher than a whisper as he drew me against him.

"There's only traces of the hormone," Dr. Atani said cautiously. "But there wasn't any before. Between that and the absence of menstruation, I am fairly confident that Neera is pregnant."

I couldn't describe the happy shout that emanated from me. I threw myself into Echo's arms. He all but lifted me up. I wrapped my legs around his waist and arms around his neck as he crushed my lips with a kiss. He spun around in place while covering my face with kisses.

Dr. Atani's gentle voice calling us finally brought us out

of the euphoria that had swept us away. Both of us felt slightly embarrassed as Echo put me back down on my feet. But my sheepish grin faded at the sight of the doctor's serious expression.

"Why are you looking at me like this?" I asked fearfully. "Is there a problem with the baby?"

She raised her palms in an appeasing gesture. "There is no sign of any problem for now. Like I said, there are only traces of CG, which leads me to believe you are barely a week along in this pregnancy. Normally, it takes between seven to fifteen days after conception for this hormone to first appear. The problem is that the mutation is very hard on the human body. Every awakening woman that has ever come to us pregnant ended up miscarrying."

"No!" I said, covering my stomach with my hand in a protective gesture.

"There's no reason to panic yet," the doctor added quickly. "Your situation isn't the same AT ALL. These women came to us already pregnant with a purely human child. Once their internal mutation began, it systematically aborted the fetus. But you conceived AFTER your evolution had begun, and it's a Sikarian child. Frankly, I don't understand how your body was ready enough to even be able to become pregnant by Echo."

"Are we going to lose it?" Echo asked in a tense voice.

Dr. Atani sighed. "I'm not going to lie or make you promises I can't swear to. This is unknown territory for all of us. It's too early to say, but the fact that you were able to conceive is promising, especially at this stage. I rushed to come here because, judging by your stats, Neera, you should enter your third phase any day now. Unlike other awakening humans, you never stopped evolving between phases. I think that's why you were able to become pregnant. The next few days will be the real test."

"So, what are we going to do?" I asked.

"For now, I want us to begin the nanobot treatment immediately to stall the evolution of your lungs and gills," she said firmly. "We will let the rest of your mutation evolve normally while we closely monitor you. I will remain on Triton at least until the entire process is complete to make sure you're fine."

"Thank you, we really appreciate it," Echo said, before casting a sheepish look at Adva. "It's not that we doubt Adva's ability to look after Neera but having an expert on the subject is reassuring."

Adva gave him a gentle smile. "Believe me, I'm just as relieved as you are. I'm grateful for any help we can get in making sure Neera will be fine."

It was my turn to smile at the healer, despite the emotional turmoil raging inside me.

"Okay, let's do it," I said.

One look at Echo confirmed he was still onboard with this. The procedure turned out to be quick and painless: two quick injections with a hypospray, one on the gills on each side of my neck, and then inhaling the seemingly invisible contents of a vial. It took less than a minute for the nanobots to reach their respective destination and go to work.

"For you, there should be absolutely no difference. You should not feel their presence or any type of discomfort," Dr. Atani explained. "If you do at any point, or feel any kind of irritation, tell us right away. Either way, we will be closely monitoring you. We'll get you through this."

CHAPTER 19
ECHO

As Dr. Atani had correctly guessed, Neera entered her third phase two days later. The wretched thing lasted an entire blasted week. I was going insane with worry. Twice my traitor of a mother slipped a sedative in my food to force me to sleep.

Mother and Raen were taking turns strumming for Neera whenever I rested, whether by choice or coercion. Obviously, I trusted them to look after my mate, but I'd never felt so anxious in my life.

On top of fearing for my mate's welfare, I was terrified of losing the baby. But the CG hormone was growing steadily in her blood, erasing any doubt as far as her being indeed pregnant.

But why was her third phase taking so long? Normally, a phase lasted about 48 hours. Her previous one had taken three days. However, it was only on the fourth day that the bumps of Neera's dome began forming on her forehead, hailing her impending ability to use echolocation. The next day, her upper arm fins came out, delicate and translucent in this early stage.

These steady, visible changes and her positive stats kept me from going mad when that phase didn't show any intention of ending.

Around noon on the sixth day, I nearly had a stroke when Neera mind-spoke to me. For a moment, I thought she had awakened and called my name, but she was still blissfully unconscious. It had been accidental, the words not really coherent in her sleep. It occurred a few more times over the next twenty-four hours. As the sun began to set on the seventh day, I seriously started to worry when Neera still didn't wake.

"It doesn't seem normal that it should take this long," I said to the doctor. "What else is still happening inside of her?"

Dr. Atani smiled at me sympathetically. "Based on our last scans, Neera's evolution is complete. Everything looks good. Her body and the baby are both doing fine. We just need to be patient for a little bit longer. Neera will awaken in her own time, when she's ready."

I wanted to insist and ask when that would be, but the doctor obviously didn't have the answer to that. I sucked it up and resumed the excruciating waiting game. At least, the nanobots were showing no negative side effects and had successfully stalled the further mutation of her gills and lungs. Then again, a part of me was beginning to wonder if that could be the thing keeping her from waking. What if her body demanded to fully complete the process?

On the eighth morning, I woke up abruptly to a tingling and slightly burning sensation in my eyes. My eyelids popped open, and my tears welled at the sight of the glow around my face reflecting on the golden scales on Neera's shoulder. Moments later, Neera stirred. She sighed then raised her hand to rub at her eyes. She turned around to face me, blinking. A quivering smile stretched my lips while my heart filled to bursting with emotion as she also stared at me with luminous eyes.

"Your eyes are glowing," she said in a whisper.

"As are yours, my love," I replied.

"Is that why they tingle?" she asked.

"Yes. It only happens once, when two Sikarian soulmates meet for the first time," I said, making no effort to hide the emotions overwhelming me.

"We're soulmates," she whispered with awe.

"Yes, we are. Now that you are who you were always meant to be, we've finally recognized each other," I said, drawing her closer against me.

She beamed at me. "That's wonderful. I knew it in my heart. But this is—" Her smile suddenly faded, worry replacing it. "My mutation is over. The baby?"

"It's fine," I said reassuringly. "You took your sweet time to come out of this blasted thing, but you are both fine. Dr. Atani said your mutation is done, and that you are perfect. The nanobots are working perfectly as well."

She squealed and gave me a bone crushing hug that had me chuckling, before she silenced it with a passionate kiss. A burning, all-consuming desire immediately surged within me. Pushing Neera onto her back, I took control of the kiss, my hands feverishly roaming over her body. She responded with equal heat. Just as I was breaking the kiss to go nibble on the sensitive spot at the base of her ear, a loud rumbling sound startled us both.

I lifted my head to cast an inquisitive look at my mate. Her stunned expression shifted to an embarrassed one.

"I believe that was my stomach saying that the baby and I need food," she said sheepishly.

I burst out laughing, the haze of lust giving way to guilt

that I hadn't immediately focused on her needs instead of yielding to my desire.

"Let's go feed you," I said, jumping out of bed and leading her after me towards the kitchen.

Another loud rumbling of her stomach appeared to signal its approval of my statement, which had us both chuckling.

I gave Neera some fruits to hold her off while I prepared something more substantial. She devoured them in no time, then looked at me expectantly, while shifting restlessly in her seat. It was both endearing and thrilling. There were no words to describe just how much I loved taking care of my mate. And now, I had two people to take care of and feed.

My child... my first little fingerling.

Like every Thalan, I'd hoped for such a blessing knowing the chances were slim. Now, I had two miracles in one: a soulmate and an offspring.

Making haste, I finished preparing breakfast and brought it to the table. Although I'd made more than enough for both of us, I barely ate anything, too busy staring at my mate with a stupid grin while she gorged with hearty vigor. My Neera... She was so beautiful, so perfect.

"Hey, there's something different about your eyes," Neera said, frowning. "Like a golden ring around your irises that wasn't there before."

I grinned and nodded. "Just like you now have one around yours." I chuckled when she recoiled. "It is called a halo—the rings that tell the whole world that we've connected with our soulmate. It is a permanent, visual sign of our bond."

"Nice! It's like a physiological wedding ring," Neera said.

I nodded.

Between two bites, she questioned me about the third phase she'd just completed. I gave her the highlights and how, now that her dome had formed, we would start her echolocation training.

Neera finished chewing her last bite, and pushed back her plate, looking quite full and sated.

"On a side note, two days ago, you started randomly mind-speaking to me," I said affectionately.

Neera froze, her beautiful eyes widening in shock. "Really? What did I say?"

"Nothing that made sense," I replied with a sympathetic smile. "But that's normal. You weren't conscious."

"Oh wow! I want to try it now! How do I do this?" she asked enthusiastically.

I shook my head. "First, we need to go see Adva and Dr. Atani to make sure you're fine. Then we can go play with your new abilities."

"Awww come on! Just two minutes! We can go see them after!" she pleaded.

"No. I know you. Two minutes will turn into a half hour or more. When you latch on, you don't let go," I gently chastised her.

She made as if to argue further, then changed her mind. Her shoulders slouched, and she pushed out her bottom lip in the most irresistible pout, while looking at me with an air of utter misery. I burst out laughing and battled the urge to lean forward in order to nip at that lip.

"You have no shame whatsoever," I exclaimed, now certain beyond any doubt that she was deliberately using that pouty lip to manipulate me. "You know I can't resist when you make that face."

She opened wide, falsely innocent eyes as she stared at me, unrepentant. "I have no idea what you're talking about. But did it work?"

I laughed again and shook my head in discouragement while she batted her eyelashes at me. Blast, how I loved her.

"Fine, but two minutes. *No more!*" I grumbled with false severity.

"WEEEE!" she squealed, clapping her hands. "So, how do I do that?"

"You must find your inner voice," I explained. "The same way your brain tells your vocal cords to produce the sounds for the words your mouth will speak, it must tell your inner voice to speak instead. It's pretty much like when you try to breathe through your gills instead of your nose. You must rewire your brain to choose which one to use."

Neera scrunched her face, her enthusiasm dampened. "In other words, you're saying this is going to be another pain in the ass to master, right?"

I chuckled, torn between amusement and sympathy. "I told you it would take more than two minutes."

"But with my gills, I have something tangible to focus on. Where's my inner voice located? What do I tell my brain to activate?" she asked, sounding a little discouraged.

"It's located in the center of your brain. Try to imagine a central point behind your eyes, right in the middle. If you focus enough, you will feel a small tingle."

She looked at me as if I was speaking gibberish but then focused and gave it a try. The seconds stretched while a growing air of frustration settled on her face. Just when I thought she was going to give up, Neera's face suddenly lit up.

"Oooh! I think I got it! It feels much higher and closer to the front than the center of my brain, but I'm definitely feeling something. Wait, I'm going to try and say 'hello' to you," she said, her enthusiasm returning in force.

Higher and closer to the front?

The question no sooner popped up in my head than a sense of dread washed over me. Horrified, I opened my mouth to warn Neera to stop, but never had a chance to speak. Time slowed to a trickle when the sonic boom resonated inside the house. I cried out as a vicious stabbing pain slashed through my eardrums. But my shout was silenced when the ensuing shockwave knocked the wind out of me.

I flew backwards as if I'd been struck in the chest by a battering ram. The table went careening to my left, as if Neera had kicked it away from her. The left-over dishes and our drinks splattered the wall, half a second before the windows exploded. I landed hard on the floor, glass shards raining on me as I covered my damaged ears.

I clenched my teeth while fighting through the ringing in my ears. I vaguely heard Neera shouting my name, but the sound was muffled, as if I was hearing her underwater. Curled up on my side, I felt Neera pulling away my chair still tangled in my legs then crouching next to me.

A bright light blinded me. Through blurred vision, I saw a tall silhouette irrupt into the house. Raen... Multiple panicked voices overlapped each other before I blacked out.

CHAPTER 20
NEERA

What the fuck had I done? What the hell had just happened? I felt faint at the sight of my husband curled up in pain on the floor. I rushed to his side, not knowing what to do. The sound of alarmed voices outside barely registered in my mind until Raen burst inside the house.

"Echo!" he exclaimed seeing his cousin on the floor and the disaster zone that the room had turned into. He cast a horrified and inquisitive look my way as he came to crouch next to Echo. "Neera, what in the world happened here?"

"I... I don't know. I was trying to mind-speak and everything exploded. Is he okay?" I asked in a total panic. Then Echo lost consciousness. "No! No! Echo, wake up! Wake up!"

"Stop, Neera," Raen said in a firm voice, placing a hand on my arm to stop me from shaking Echo. "He just passed out."

"Oh dear," Dr. Atani whispered as she entered the room.

"Please, help him!" I pleaded.

"Let me guess," the doctor said as she came to Echo's side

and ran her handheld scanner over him. "You tried echoloca-tion or mind-speak?"

"Mind-speak," I said in a trembling voice.

"Of course," she said, shaking her head. "I should have warned you beforehand that this could happen, but I thought we would have talked before you attempted any of your new abilities."

Even though I'd been the one to hurt Echo, the doctor's tone implied self-recrimination.

"He wanted me to wait until I'd seen you, but I was too impatient. I'm always too damn impatient. Is he going to be okay?"

"Yes, dear. Do not worry. It happens all the time with awakening Thalans," she said in a reassuring tone. "He's going to be sore for a little bit, and it will take about two days for his hearing to return to normal. Then, he will be as good as new. Let's take him back to the clinic."

"Can I carry him, or do we need a stretcher?" Raen asked.

"Either is fine, it won't harm him," Dr. Atani said.

Half the village that hadn't yet left for work had gathered outside the house to see what the heck had happened. Raen immediately reassured them when they cast horrified looks his way as he carried an unconscious Echo. I was mortified and worried sick.

"Do not fret, Neera," Dr. Atani said in a soothing voice. "You created a sonic boom instead of using mind-speak. It happens with pretty much every awakening human. Our younglings do the same. Since they still have baby domes when they first use echolocation, they do not have the full power that an adult like you does. You will just need to take some safety measures until you master that ability."

When we entered the clinic, Dr. Atani and Adva subjected

both Echo and me to a full battery of tests. Echo regained consciousness halfway through, just in time to see his very panicked mother rushing inside the room.

The healers' reassurances apparently failed to calm Edlyn. She didn't relax until the domes of both of our medical pods opened, and she was able to talk to her son and me.

"How are you feeling, Echo?" Dr. Atani asked.

"Like I got caught in a riptide and ended up smashing into a rock wall," he said with a wince.

"I'm so sorry. I'm so very sorry," I said piteously.

"It's okay, my love," he said with a gentle smile—that failed to hide his pain. "We're all learning."

Adva gave him some painkillers that did wonders to numb the soreness, then his own nanobot treatment to repair the damage to his eardrums. Edlyn then insisted on having her own look at her son. She no sooner approached him than she froze.

"Your eyes! You have a halo!" she exclaimed.

Echo beamed at her, a shy expression settling on his face as he nodded. "This morning, when Neera woke up, we both glowed. We are soulmates."

"Oh, my loves! Congratulations! I'm so happy for you!" Edlyn said, hugging and kissing her son before doing the same to me.

After giving the baby and me a clean bill of health, we sat through the warnings and instructions from Dr. Atani.

Echo was to rest for the next forty-eight hours, no deep dives, no physical exertion. I was forbidden from even *thinking* about using mind-speak or echolocation anywhere near buildings or out of water. Once I formally began training for both of those abilities, Echo was to use ear protection and keep a minimum distance of four meters from me until I got a better control of them.

It was mortifying just how far from any building or life-form Echo took me to train those abilities in the water. Thankfully, I quickly took to mind-speak, which improved our underwater communication. With my full mutation complete, my eyes stopped messing with me when it came to using iridophores to talk. But I far preferred mind-speak as it avoided confusion, didn't require me to look in his specific direction and, above all, it provided intonation that often completely changed the meaning of the words.

However, Echo insisted that I master that ability none-theless as mind-speak could only be used with a single person at a time. Iridophores allowed group messaging which could be critical when traveling in dangerous waters with multiple people.

Echolocation, though, royally kicked my butt. Hitting the right frequency for the right purpose proved quite challenging. It wasn't like I had a knob I could turn to tune it. It basically came down to trying to learn a new musical scale when you were tone deaf. For all my complaining, detecting objects and their distance didn't turn out to be so bad. Trying to figure out their nature broke my brain. It would take time to master. Similarly, recognizing and understanding the message of a sonic pulse I received was just as tough.

Echo kept saying I was doing phenomenally well. I had no reason to doubt him. But I couldn't help wishing a magical wand would impart me all the knowledge I needed instead of this slow, painstaking process.

In truth, I now possessed too many new abilities and was trying too hard to master them all at once. The minute I caved in to Echo's repeated request that we focus on one ability, only flexing the muscles of the others for a few minutes daily so they wouldn't atrophy, I started making significant progress.

Three weeks after the end of my third phase, Echo's father Leith arrived in Soigo Reef. Holy cow, the man was smoking hot! The same way Edlyn could have passed for Echo's girlfriend or sister, Leith could have been his older brother. With Edlyn's light purple color, I had expected Leith to be a reddish or magenta color to justify Echo's pink scales—even though the hue of the offspring could be totally random. So, when Leith emerged from the water like a sunken god with the palest skin like white opal, silver white hair, and the same pale eyes as Echo, my jaw literally dropped to the ground. He was taller with broader shoulders than Echo, but according to Edlyn, my husband would grow to match his father's size as he aged.

When he showed up, Edlyn ran down the beach and threw herself into his arms. He lifted her up, twirling while she laughed and kissed his face. It was a beautiful and moving moment. But my heart ached for Seiru, one of Edlyn's other two partners, who stood by observing them. At least, there was no jealousy or sadness visible on his features as he did so. He actually seemed amused, as if he found it endearing.

"Your parents really seem to love each other," I whispered to Echo.

"They do," he said with a wistful smile. "They've been together for decades."

"Why don't they get married?" I asked.

"Because they aren't soulmates," he said matter-of-factly. "However, I believe once my mother's fertile years are behind her, she will marry him."

Seeing Edlyn and Leith coming our way, his possessive

arm wrapped around her shoulders, silenced us. I suddenly felt nervous and made a mess of trying to tuck a lock of hair behind my long, pointy fin ears, making me even more embarrassed. Leith's pale gaze never strayed from me as he closed the distance between us, a strange smile stretching his sensuous lips. Echo's resemblance with his father was undeniable.

Leith stopped right in front of me and studied my features with an intensity that had me swallowing hard. "Hello, daughter. I am Leith, Echo's sire. It is an honor to meet you at last."

I gave him a timid smile. "Hello, Leith. The honor is all mine."

He smiled. To my shock, he released Edlyn's shoulders to cup my face with both hands. "Welcome to our family," he said before leaning forward and kissing the middle dome on my forehead.

My throat tightened as I mumbled a thank you. But he didn't let go right away, his gaze locking with mine as an air of wonder descended on his features. His thumbs gently caressed the sides of my eyes before his head jerked towards his son. His lips parted in shock while Echo puffed out his chest with a proud grin.

"You're haloed," Leith whispered.

"We are," Echo replied.

Leith turned back to look at me with an unreadable expression. "You truly are a great blessing to our family, and to my only son. I hear you are also with child?"

I nodded proudly. "We're a little over five weeks. Since we knew you were coming, we decided to wait for your arrival before getting the ultrasound. We're going to hear the baby's heartbeat for the first time."

A powerful emotion crossed his features. "My dear children," he whispered before drawing both Echo and I into his embrace.

When Echo had first suggested it, I'd thought it was a cool idea. But then, I started fearing maybe Leith wouldn't be all that interested. I didn't want to be that parent who made a nuisance of themselves thinking that everyone and their brother were interested in fussing over their little bundle of joy. But his reaction confirmed it had been the right choice.

After he released us, we made our way to the clinic.

"Is he taking good care of you?" Leith asked.

Echo gave his father an outraged look. "Of course, I am!"

He gave his son a dismissive sideways glance. "I asked her, not you."

Edlyn snorted, which earned her a glaring stare from her son.

I laughed and caressed the back of Echo's shoulder in a soothing gesture. "Yes, he does. I almost feel guilty, he spoils me so much. He's slowly turning me into a spoiled brat."

"As it should be," Leith said, giving Echo a proud nod.

I shook my head, discouraged, while Edlyn winked at me. I knew then that Leith and I would get along wonderfully.

Although Dr. Atani and Adva weren't too keen on all this crowding in the room, they gave us a pass as pregnancies were such a huge deal for their people... for *our* people. I settled on the examination table, suddenly feeling nervous. Echo held my hand, looking as nervous as I did, while his parents seemed to struggle to contain their excitement.

Dr. Atani slightly lowered my veil and applied the gel before starting the ultrasound. My hand tightened around Echo's when the image appeared on the screen. I had no real idea what I was looking at, but Adva and Dr. Atani both tensing had my anxiety skyrocketing.

"No way!" the doctor whispered, eyes wide in shock.

"What? What's wrong?" I asked, on the verge of panic.

Edlyn and Echo gasped, the two of them seeming to also understand what was going on. As they both also had a biology background, they could see things Leith and I couldn't.

"No, it's... Hang on," the doctor said distractedly.

She tapped on the interface of the ultrasound device, and a pulsing sound filled the room. It sounded odd, like a horse galloping, but with its steps faltering.

"Is that the baby's heart?" I asked, my voice rising in pitch as I was getting ready to freak out. "Why does it sound like that? Is it normal for a Thalan? What—?"

"No, my love," Echo said, tears of joy welling in his eyes. His gaze flicked towards the healers. "Is this what I think I'm hearing and seeing?"

"Yes, Echo," Adva said, looking just as emotional. "It is."

"IT'S WHAT?!" I shouted, losing my shit.

"Our twins," Echo said. "This sound is their overlapping heartbeats. And these two dots on the monitor are our little ones."

I froze as Dr. Atani moved the ultrasound over my belly to focus on one of the two dots. The sound of the second heart-beat faded in the background, making this fetus' single pulse clearer.

I didn't realize I had started crying before my vision became too blurry to clearly read the monitor. I vaguely heard Leith shout out with joy, while Edlyn, Adva, and Dr. Atani laughed. But none of that mattered to me. I was lost in the loving embrace of my mate and the sound of our babies' heartbeats going strong.

EPILOGUE
NEERA

The news spread like wildfire, in large part thanks to Leith—not that we had planned on hiding it from anyone. But seeing my father-in-law strutting about like a proud peacock cracked me up to no end. You'd think he had a hand in my pregnancy. Finding out that this was a Thalan first certainly put a different perspective on things. They never had twins, be they identical or fraternal.

Needless to say that Dr. Atani begged me to grant her permission to use my data, including samples, to further their own research. She believed I could help them get closer to resolving their reproductive issues. Naturally, I said yes.

But if I thought Echo had been majorly protective before, things reached a whole new level now. Worse still, his dad, Raen, Ouren, and Opire joined the fray. Then the entire freaking village, too. There was *always* someone lurking around, looking after me. The more inconspicuous they tried to be about it, the more obvious it was.

As much as it annoyed me, I couldn't even get mad. Pregnancies were too few and far between for them to play around whenever someone finally managed to conceive. With their youthful appearance and long lifespan, one was easily fooled into thinking their population was younger than in reality.

The following week, when a purple moon rose in the darkening sky of Triton, Echo had us riding peridorns towards the Liamera Abyss, a great distance from the village. We made a few detours along the way to avoid the dangerous sectors where predators roamed. As we approached our destination, he told me to use my echolocation to find a large seashell, one more or less shaped like a scallop shell.

Intrigued, I complied. While far from mastering that skill, I could now distinguish shapes fairly clearly, differentiate a series of materials, identify a number of creatures, and even estimate the time to reach them based on the distance.

It took me far less time than I would have imagined to detect not just one shell, but an entire field of them. We dismounted our peridorns, and I followed Echo into what normally was the darkest pit in this section of the ocean. But not tonight. The entire edge of the abyss was lit up by a myriad of bioluminescent creatures—or were they plants?—lining it. Some twinkled like stars, lighting the way into the fathomless depths. Wedged in between them, large shells, at least fifty centimeters wide, protruded from the edges.

"They are called asenief shells," Echo mind-spoke to me. *"They only open to the light of a purple moon."*

As if prompted by his words, the asenief shells began opening one after the other, like a wave. Within, instead of the scallop or mussel-like creature I'd expected to see, sat an adorable creature resembling a dumbo octopus with the colorful and bumpy skin of a nudibranch.

"They are our version of the human's wishing wells," Echo continued while removing something from his small

arm pouch. He then showed it to me. *"Instead of tossing a coin, you feed it this very rare mineral called feglite after making a wish. The upside is that you immediately get an answer to your wish. Or rather, I should say to the blessing you want to bestow."*

"Really?" I exclaimed, stunned and fascinated. *"How does it respond?"*

"It will secrete a gem back to you," Echo explained. *"The color of the gem will determine what outcome you will get. Usually, this stone is used by soulmates—if they are lucky enough to find each other—or by couples considering marriage to ask for a blessing of their union. This feglite stone was Raen's wedding gift to us. But you can cast the blessing on anything or anyone else you wish."*

"Wow, that is so generous of him," I said, my heart filling with affection for the male I'd grown to consider as a baby brother. *"But what kind of blessings do the aseniefs grant?"*

"Happiness, health, prosperity, fertility, longevity, wisdom, and luck."

My eyes widened in surprise. *"Not love?"*

"The couples are usually soulmates. Love is already guaranteed," Echo said with a smile.

"Right. That makes sense."

"So, pick a shell and bestow a blessing," he said, placing the stone in my hand.

I swam around the abyss, looking at the various aseniefs, hoping one would somehow call to me. And then one of them did. Its pinkish color with reddish bumps on its skin almost matched Echo's colors. It blinked its big, beady eyes at me and bobbed again. I didn't hesitate.

I wasn't the superstitious type, but this felt too special, too solemn not to take it very seriously. My instinctive thought was to ask for the asenief to bless my marriage to Echo. But I rapidly dismissed that idea. Our marriage was already blessed in all the ways I could have dreamed of. I was in love with the most perfect man, who also happened to be my soulmate.

I considered casting it on Raen that he should find his soulmate. Then on Edlyn and Leith so that they could have that second child they so longed for. But then I thought of my unborn twins. They were healthy—so far. However, I couldn't deny feeling some level of apprehension as to how they would fare after their births. I had such a rough go at life, and they'd been conceived when I technically shouldn't have been able to. What if they were born full Sikarians and this atmosphere didn't agree with them?

That sealed it.

I would like a blessing for my children, so that they may thrive and be happy throughout their lives.

As soon as I formed the wish in my head, I extended the piece of feglite to the asenief. The tiny protrusion in front of its face shot out almost like an elephant's trunk to absorb the stone. Its round little body wiggled, as if the creature was swaying to a song only it could hear. Its semi-translucent skin appeared to glow from within as it closed its eyes, apparently savoring the treat. I sat there transfixed, mesmerized by the shifting colors of the asenief. And then it stilled.

Its eyes blinked open, and its tiny trunk undulated before spitting out two small gems in quick succession. Faster than light, Echo caught them, carefully opening his palms for us to look at them. Red, tear-drop-shaped, the gems appeared to have captured a constellation of stars within.

Echo snorted then smiled upon seeing them.

"What does it mean?" I asked through mind-speak.

"Confirmation of the blessing we've already received,"

Echo said. *"This color and shape mean fertility. And it gave us two, confirming our marriage will be blessed with twins."*

I frowned and shook my head. *"I didn't ask for a blessing for us. I asked for one for our unborn children."*

Echo's eyes widened, then his smile broadened. *"Then both of our children will be fertile!"*

In the upcoming weeks, these famous words took on a whole new meaning. At the fourteen-week mark, one week before she was scheduled to leave Triton, Dr. Atani performed the 'gender reveal' ultrasound. I was carrying twin girls. That revelation convinced her to remain on Triton until I gave birth.

The village went insane. If they'd been overly protective before, everyone went crazy with this information. As my baby bump grew, people—especially the females—would caress it in passing as if it was some sort of fertility talisman. Frankly, it got to the point where I almost expected the males to start groping Echo's balls for some of that 'golden seed' magic.

We even started receiving gifts for the girls from complete strangers from other cities, mainly toys. Leith, who was an architect and a builder, spent an entire month building a dwelling for Echo and me in the sunken city. One of the city crafters offered to turn our wish gems into necklaces for each of our girls.

To my dismay, in the last weeks of my pregnancy, I developed major cravings for perleen fish—which my esophageal teeth approved of—and for the repulsive ubrils. As much as the thought of eating finned magots grossed me out, I couldn't deny the wretched things were actually quite tasty. They vaguely tasted like crab legs. Naturally, Echo took great pleasure in teasing me about it.

The delivery went off without a hitch. My girls were beautiful, with their father's pale eyes, a perfect mix of my face and his, the generic peach skin color of all young Thalan offspring, but beautiful burgundy patterns along the edges of their tail membranes that hinted at the stunning color their scales would turn as they reached puberty.

We named the firstborn Sanya and the second one Ethea. Unlike human babies, they didn't cry at birth. They emitted instead a whistling sound that quickly evolved into their siren songs.

As I would quickly find out, Thalan babies were master manipulators. When they were hungry or needed a poopy diaper changed, they didn't make noise. They sang at a frequency too high for us to consciously perceive. But it irresistibly lured us to them. I'd be in the middle of studying the material for my marine veterinary degree, then suddenly find myself entering the nursery, not even remembering making my way there. And my girls would be grinning their gums at me and waving their tiny, webbed hands and feet to be picked up.

"Sorry," Echo said with a sheepish expression while holding Ethea. "I was hoping they would let you work in peace. I changed their diapers, played with them, and even tried to bottle feed them, but to no avail."

"That's because your daughters are divas from being excessively spoiled by their father," I said pointedly while picking up Sanya and settling in my feeding chair. "Bottled milk is beneath them. Isn't it, little princess?"

Sanya didn't bother responding, her greedy mouth latching on to my left breast. Echo approached me, looking totally unremorseful as he settled Ethea on my right side so they could feed at the same time. As soon as they were both in position, eyes closed as they fed, my girls reached out for each other, their tiny hands intertwining between my breasts.

My heart swelled for my babies, and I kissed the top of their heads in turn.

"Thrice blessed," Echo said looking at us. "I love you, my mate."

"I love you too, Echo."

THE END

ECHO

ECHO

DARTER RAY

ASENIEF

ALSO BY REGINE ABEL

THE VEREDIAN CHRONICLES
Escaping Fate
Blind Fate
Raising Amalia
Twist of Fate
Hands of Fate
Defying Fate

BRAXIANS
Anton's Grace
Ravik's Mercy
Krygor's Hope

XIAN WARRIORS
Doom
Legion
Raven
Bane
Chaos
Varnog
Reaper
Wrath
Xenon

PRIME MATING AGENCY
I Married A Lizardman
I Married A Naga
I Married A Birdman
I Married A Merman

THE MIST
The Mistwalker
The Nightmare

BLOOD MAIDENS OF KARTHIA
Claiming Thalia

VALOS OF SONHADRA
Unfrozen
Iced

EMPATHS OF LYRIA
An Alien For Christmas

THE SHADOW REALMS
Dark Swan

OTHER
True As Steel
Bluebeard's Curse
Alien Awakening
Heart of Stone
The Hunchback

ABOUT REGINE

USA Today bestselling author Regine Abel is a fantasy, paranormal and sci-fi junky. Anything with a bit of magic, a touch of the unusual, and a lot of romance will have her jumping for joy. She loves creating hot alien warriors and no-nonsense, kick-ass heroines that evolve in fantastic new worlds while embarking on action-packed adventures filled with mystery and the twists you never saw coming.

Before devoting herself as a full-time writer, Regine had surrendered to her other passions: music and video games! After a decade working as a Sound Engineer in movie dubbing and live concerts, Regine became a professional Game Designer and Creative Director, a career that has led her from her home in Canada to the US and various countries in Europe and Asia.

Facebook
https://www.facebook.com/regine.abel.author/

Website
https://regineabel.com

Regine's Rebels Reader Group
https://www.facebook.com/groups/ReginesRebels/

Newsletter
http://smarturl.it/RA_Newsletter

Goodreads
http://smarturl.it/RA_Goodreads

Bookbub
https://www.bookbub.com/profile/regine-abel

Amazon
http://smarturl.it/AuthorAMS